Jennifer Taylor has written for several different Mills & Boon series, but it wasn't until she 'discovered' Medical Romances that she found her true niche. Jennifer loves the blend of modern romance and exciting medical drama. Widowed, she divides her time between homes in Lancashire and the Lake District. Her hobbies include reading, walking, travelling and spending time with her two gorgeous grandchildren.

Also by Jennifer Taylor

One More Night with Her Desert Prince...
Best Friend to Perfect Bride
Miracle Under the Mistletoe
The Greek Doctor's Secret Son
Reawakened by the Surgeon's Touch

The Larches Practice miniseries

The Boss Who Stole Her Heart
Bride for the Single Dad
Reunited by Their Baby

Discover more at millsandboon.co.uk.

REUNITED BY THEIR BABY

JENNIFER TAYLOR

MILLS & BOON

First published in Great Britain 2018
by Mills & Boon, an imprint of HarperCollins*Publishers*
1 London Bridge Street, London, SE1 9GF

Large Print edition 2018

© 2018 Jennifer Taylor

ISBN: 978-0-263-07304-1

MIX
Paper from
responsible sources
FSC
www.fsc.org
FSC™ C007454

This book is produced from independently certified
FSC™ paper to ensure responsible forest management. For
more information visit www.harpercollins.co.uk/green.

Printed and bound in Great Britain
by CPI Group (UK) Ltd, Croydon, CR0 4YY

For the other members of the earring club:
Charlotte, Janet and Ruth. With thanks
for all the fun and laughter.

Special thanks must go to Ruth for her
'research'. Above and beyond, is all I can say!

CHAPTER ONE

HE WAS LATE. Almost a year late by his reckoning, although, by rights, he should have been here from the very beginning.

Callum O'Neill's mouth thinned as he paid off the cab and turned to face the cottage that had once been his home. He had sworn when he had left that he would never come back here again. This place held too many bad memories and he had promised himself that he would do his best to forget what had gone on. However, that had been before he had received that letter. Before everything had changed.

Callum could feel his heart thumping as he walked up the path. He knocked on the door, wondering what sort of reception he would receive. He wasn't expecting red carpet treatment but he was hoping that things would improve once he explained what had happened. It had taken months for the letter to reach him. He had been moving around such a lot as he had helped to set up the programme he had been working on. It was vital to roll it out to as many communities as possible as Malaria was endemic over much of sub-Saharan Africa. It was little wonder the letter hadn't reached him for such a long time but would Beth understand that? He hoped so. He couldn't bear to think that they would end up arguing again. They had done enough of that in the past and he, for one, couldn't bear to go down that route again.

'If you're wanting Dr Andrews then she isn't there.'

Callum swung round. 'Oh, right. Do you know where she is, by any chance?' he asked, recognising the elderly woman who had spoken to him as a patient from the surgery. He had worked at The Larches Surgery for almost a year, filling in as a locum GP so he could be with Beth. Their relationship had already been under a lot of strain by then and it hadn't helped that they were living so far apart—he based in London and Beth in the Yorkshire Dales—so he had made the decision to relocate. Sadly, it hadn't helped their marriage as much as he had hoped it would. Things had gone too far by that stage and so instead they had split up, which made what had happened later all the more poignant…

'Why, she's in the church, of course! Where else would she be?' The woman frowned. 'You're Dr O'Neill, aren't you? I thought I recognised you. We've not seen you around here for a while. Funny that you should turn up today, although maybe you've been invited.'

'Invited?' Callum repeated uncertainly. 'Invited to what?'

'The wedding.' She sniffed. 'Although if you ask me it's far too soon for them to be getting married. I mean, they barely know each other. Still, fools rush in, as my old mum used to say.'

With that, she went on her way. Callum stared after her, feeling shock reverberating throughout his entire body. Beth was getting married again? She was getting married *today*! His feet were already moving before the thought had sunk in. He raced across the road, taking the path that led to Beesdale Parish Church. He could hear the church bells ringing and put on a spurt. He had to make Beth see that she couldn't go ahead and marry someone else, not now, not ever! It was as though his mind was crystal clear all of a sudden and for the first time in ages he knew what he wanted, and that was Beth.

The bells had stopped ringing by the time Callum reached the church and his panic increased to epic proportions. The service must have started and he had no idea how long it took to reach the part where the minister declared the couple man and wife. When he and Beth had married it was in a registry office, a no-frills affair that had been over in minutes.

Neither of them had cared about the ceremony. The only thing that had mattered was that they could make their vows to love and cherish each other for the rest of their lives. They had been so sure that their love would last for ever, he thought sadly, but it hadn't worked out that way. As he had discovered, all the promises in the world couldn't guarantee that.

The thought lent wings to his feet as he raced up the path. The heavy oak doors were closed and he wasted valuable seconds, wrestling them open. He almost fell into the church when they finally gave way and he saw people turn to look at him but he had eyes for no one except the woman in white standing before the altar. She was the only person who hadn't turned around and his heart ached with a searing pain when it struck him that she was oblivious to his presence. She was too busy looking at the man she was about to marry to notice him.

Callum felt the coldness of defeat sweep over him. In that moment, he realised that he had no right to stop what was happening. He turned to leave, knowing it was the only thing he could do. He'd had his chance and blown it; it wasn't fair to expect Beth to take him back. Maybe he hadn't known the truth until that letter had reached him but he had still left her, hadn't he? Why would she want him back when she had found someone else?

'Callum? What are you *doing* here?'

He recognised her voice immediately, heaven knew, he should do when he heard it every night in his dreams. Each time he fell asleep he heard her speaking to him, saw her, touched her, held her, loved her, felt her love him in return. The only difference was that she wouldn't be looking at him with love in her eyes now. Her love was reserved for another man, the man who was going to do his best to make her happy, as he had failed to do.

'I asked you a question, Callum. At least have the decency to answer it!'

There was no welcome in her voice, no hint

of warmth. That she didn't want him there was obvious. Callum turned slowly around because what else could he do? Just for a moment his vision blurred before he managed to focus and he blinked as he took stock of the pale pink dress she was wearing and the jaunty little hat with its swirl of purple feathers on the crown…

His gaze flew to the couple standing in front of the altar and he felt the blood drain from his head when he realised that the bride was Polly. He didn't recognise the groom; he had never seen him before, but it didn't matter. The only thing that mattered was that Beth wasn't getting married today. It meant that he still had a chance, one precious chance to win her back! His heart was in his mouth as he turned to face her. This was the most important moment of his life and he had to get it right.

'I came to see you, Beth. You and our baby.'

Beth could feel her legs trembling and clutched hold of a nearby pew. She could hear the mur-

mur of voices as the congregation started whispering together. Were they as shocked as she was to see Callum? Were they wondering why he was here and what he wanted? In a small town like Beesdale, it was hard to keep anything secret—everyone knew that he had run out on her and left her pregnant. Now the thought of her daughter helped to steady her. No way was she going to allow Callum to destroy Beatrix's life the way he had destroyed hers!

She turned cold hazel eyes on him. 'Come outside. We can't talk in here.'

She didn't wait to see if he was following as she led the way out of the church. It was up to Callum what he did and she had no intention of trying to influence him in any way. She walked down the path, only pausing when she reached the lich gate. There was very little traffic about as most of the townspeople were in the church. Polly was the local midwife and greatly loved; everyone wanted to help her celebrate her special day. Tears suddenly pricked her eyes but

Beth blinked them away. She wasn't going to think about the dreams she'd had when she and Callum had married. That was all in the past and too much had happened since. Their divorce had been difficult enough, but the fact that he hadn't even bothered to acknowledge their child until today was so much worse.

'I'm sorry. I know it isn't enough but I am truly sorry, Beth.'

There was a note in his deep voice that tugged at her heart strings before she pulled herself together. If she gave in and allowed her emotions free rein then she would regret it. She had to focus on the facts, highlight them in neon-bright letters so she would never forget them. Callum had left her. He had left her because he hadn't loved her any more. He had been so desperate to be rid of her that he hadn't even contacted her when she had written to tell him that she was pregnant. He could apologise all he liked, but it wouldn't change anything.

'It's too late for apologies, Callum. I'm not interested. The only thing I want to know is what you're doing here.'

'Surely that's obvious,' he shot back. 'I came to see you and the baby.'

'I see. And it's taken you—what?—over a year to get round to it?' She gave a little laugh, hoping he couldn't hear the bitterness it held. There must be no displays of emotion, no hint of any feelings that might make him think that she still cared. 'You didn't exactly rush to get here, did you? But there again, I doubt if Beatrix and I were your number one priority—'

'Beatrix? You mean that we have a daughter?'

'Yes,' Beth replied curtly, closing her mind to the shock she could hear in his voice. If she refused to admit to her own feelings then she certainly didn't want to wonder how Callum felt!

Callum felt his head reel. Ever since he had read Beth's letter he had wondered about the sex of their baby. To be honest, it had been difficult to believe that he was finally about to become a father after everything they had been through, yet all of a sudden finding out that they had a little girl made it seem real. His breath caught as he was swamped by a whole host of emotions ranging from shock to sheer elation. He had a daughter. A little girl called Beatrix. The thought seemed to rock his whole world so that it was hard to speak. 'H-how old is she?'

'Almost ten months,' Beth replied tightly. 'Although if you hadn't been so busy saving the world then you wouldn't need to ask that, Callum.'

'That isn't true!' He ran his hands through his thick dark brown hair, feeling them trembling as he tried to picture what Beatrix looked like. Was she dark like him or fair like Beth? It was impossible to guess and before he could ask, Beth carried on.

'Oh, I think it is true, but you just don't want to admit it.' She stared back at him, unwilling to give him the benefit of the doubt. Even though he understood why she refused to accept that he was telling the truth, it still hurt. 'If you'd cared back then, you would have contacted me. Even a text message would have been better than nothing, but you couldn't even spare the time for that. The fact that I was expecting our child meant nothing to you, did it, Callum?'

'Of course it did!' He grasped hold of her hands, his fingers biting into hers as he willed her to believe him. 'It was what we'd wanted for so long, Beth. What we'd struggled to achieve...'

He broke off, obviously recalling what a struggle it had been, Beth thought sadly. She had always wanted a family. Coming from a close and loving family herself, she had never even considered the idea that conceiving a child of her own might prove to be a problem. With two older sisters, who both had children, she had simply assumed that she would have them too. However, as the months had passed, and she had failed to get pregnant, it had seemed increasingly unlikely that she would ever achieve her dream of becoming a mother.

Callum had never been as keen on the idea of them having a child, however. Although he had gone along with her desire to have a baby, she knew it had been more to please her than out of a genuine need to have a family of his own. She had told herself that it didn't matter, that he would love their child every bit as much as she did when it arrived. She had been so sure it was the right thing for them to do that she had set aside her doubts when the consultant had suggested they try fertility treatment.

Had she been wrong to do so? she wondered suddenly. Wrong to force him into a course of action that he had been reluctant to take? There was no doubt that the strain of keeping to the gruelling regime had put intense pressure on their relationship. Lovemaking had changed from being an expression of their feelings for each other to a duty, passion no longer dictated by their mutual desire but by the readings on a thermometer.

Was it any wonder that Callum had resented

it? That they had argued? With the benefit of hindsight, Beth could see that there had been faults on both sides, but it didn't alter the fact that it had been Callum who had called a halt, Callum who had decided that he didn't want to be with her any more, Callum who had asked her for a divorce. If he had loved her, *really* loved her, then he would never have left her. He would have stayed.

CHAPTER TWO

CALLUM COULD FEEL his insides quivering. First there was the shock of thinking that Beth was getting married again and now this. Her hostility was palpable even though he could tell that she was doing her best not to show how angry she felt. That in itself hurt because she had never hidden her feelings before. Whatever Beth had felt, she had been completely open about it.

When she had fallen in love with him, she hadn't tried to hide it, the same as she hadn't tried to hide her distress when their marriage had ended. To know that he was responsible for such a change in her was incredibly painful but he couldn't allow himself to be sidetracked. He had come here for a specific purpose and he had to focus on that. Beth wasn't going to believe a word he said unless he managed to convince her that he was telling the truth.

'Look, Beth, I know how it must appear but the situation isn't as straightforward as you think,' he began.

'Save it, Callum. I've already told you that I'm not interested.' Her tone was cold, indifferent even, and something inside him died a little. Even anger was preferable to this total lack of interest. 'You've had months to contact me and never bothered. So why should I listen to you now just because you've suddenly decided it's time we talked?'

'Because you don't understand!'

He let go of her hands, feeling the pain of her rejection biting deep into his soul. Heaven knew, he had enough experience of being rejected to recognise it. His parents had never really wanted him. They had both been high-flyers, dedicated to their work, and his unscheduled arrival had been viewed as a disruption to their busy lives.

He had been brought up by a succession of nannies until he was old enough to be sent away to boarding school. Holidays had been a nightmare; both his mother and his father had made it clear that they resented having to waste time entertaining him. It had been a relief to them all when he had been old enough to go away on his own. Skiing trips, diving holidays—he'd done the lot and enjoyed them too. At least he hadn't felt like a burden. People were being paid to look after him and that made it easier.

The ties had been completely severed by the time he went to university. Apart from the obligatory birthday and Christmas cards, he had no contact with them these days. He didn't miss them; it was impossible to miss something he had never had.

However, they had taught him a valuable lesson, which was that no one should have a child unless they were prepared to put it first. That was why he'd had reservations when Beth had suggested they should have a baby. He had been afraid that he wouldn't measure up as a parent, that the genes he had inherited would affect his ability to be a proper father to their child, but he had allowed himself to be persuaded because it was what Beth had wanted so desperately.

Would he have agreed if he'd had any idea how hard it would be? he wondered suddenly. How agonising it would be to watch her suffer such terrible disappointment, month after month, when she had failed to get pregnant? Of course he wouldn't! He had loved her to distraction and it was unthinkable that he would have allowed her to go through that kind of torment.

That was why he had called a halt and asked her for a divorce. Maybe Beth believed that he had done it for his own sake but it wasn't true. He simply couldn't bear to see her torturing herself any longer. How ironic that after all they had been through, she should have fallen pregnant that last night they had slept together.

'What is there to understand? I wrote to tell you I was pregnant and you didn't reply. That says it all.' She shrugged, her expression so cold when Callum forced his mind back to the present that he felt chilled to the bone. It was hard to believe that Beth could look at him that way.

'But I never received your letter!' he protested.

'Then why are you here?' she shot back and he felt relief surge through him when he heard the stirrings of anger in her voice. It was better to be upbraided than be treated with such indifference.

'What I meant was that I never received it for months. I was in Africa, travelling around while I helped set up a new malaria programme, and somehow it never caught up with me.' He looked deep into her eyes, willing her to believe him. 'It only reached me last month and as soon as I read it, I made arrangements to fly back to England. I got here as fast as I could, Beth—I swear.'

Beth wanted to believe him, she wanted it

with a desperation that defied all logic. She had sworn that she would never allow herself to be swayed by anything Callum said but, staring into his deep brown eyes, it was so very tempting... The sound of bells ringing broke the spell. Beth stepped back, her breath coming in fast little spurts as she realised how close she had come to breaking her own promise. Surely she had learned her lesson after what had happened between them? Learned never to believe a word Callum said? If he could tell her that he loved her and then leave her, it proved beyond any doubt how untrustworthy he was.

She swung round, ignoring him when he called her name. She didn't want to listen to him any more, didn't want to see him, to be tempted in any way at all. She had to think about Beatrix and the effect it would have on her in the future if she found out that her father was a liar.

She re-joined the wedding party, nodding when Polly asked her if she was all right. She wasn't all right, by any means, but she wouldn't say so, wouldn't ruin her friend's special day. Polly deserved this after everything she had been through. She deserved every second of happiness that came her way. She had found the man she loved and he loved her too—their future was rosy and golden and would be filled with joy. Just as hers should have been if Callum hadn't stopped loving her.

The tears came then, hot and bitter as they streamed down her face, but she wasn't the only one crying. Weddings were an emotional time and a lot of the guests were shedding a tear or two. Beth dried her eyes then took her place on the church steps while the photographs were taken, smiling and pretending to be full of joy on this happy day while inside she felt devastated and angry and so very alone.

She glanced towards the lich gate but there was no sign of Callum. Whether he would seek her out again, she had no idea. It didn't really matter. Nothing he said could make up for what he had done, no excuses about letters taking months to reach him would change things. The fact was that he had left her, left her when she had needed him most of all. And that was the only thing that counted.

Callum had managed to book himself a room in the local pub. He carried his bag up the narrow staircase and opened the bedroom door. The room was small and rather cramped with double dormer roofs taking up most of the ceiling space but he didn't care. It was somewhere to sleep tonight because one thing was certain: he wouldn't be sleeping in Beth's bed!

Frustration ate away at him as he tossed his bag onto the bed. Maybe he hadn't expected red carpet treatment but he had hoped for a better reception than that. It was obvious that Beth wasn't going to forgive him in a hurry and it made him see how foolish he'd been to hope that she would. He sighed wearily. Had he really thought that he could win her round with a few well-chosen words? That he could tell

Beth what had happened and that she would just accept it? He must have been living in cloud cuckoo land if he had!

No way was this going to be easy. He would have to work at it, gain her trust, make her understand that he hadn't ignored her or their baby, and *then* convince her that he wanted to be involved in their lives.

Fear trickled coldly down his spine at the thought. He knew nothing about what it took to be a father, did he? Most people learned the art from their own father but he certainly wasn't going to use his as a role model. He would be batting in the dark, striking out this way and that in the hope that he would somehow discover how to be a good parent. What if he failed? What if he tried his best but still couldn't measure up to the role? He couldn't bear to imagine the harm it might cause his daughter if he flunked it. His heart caught. He couldn't bear to imagine Beth's contempt either if that happened.

* * *

Beth collected Beatrix from the childminder's house and took her home. Polly had wanted her to take the baby to the church but Beth had decided not to risk it. At almost ten months old Beatrix was attempting to walk and soon became frustrated if she was made to sit still for any length of time. The thought of her daughter creating a fuss during the service had made Beth decide to leave her with Alison, the childminder. Now she was doubly glad that she had. She still wasn't sure if she was going to allow Callum to see her. After all, if he had been that interested in his daughter then he would have been in touch before now, although, according to Callum, it hadn't been his fault, had it?

The thought nagged away at her as she got Beatrix ready for bed. The little girl loved water and Beth let her splash away in the bath for longer than usual. She rarely spent any time apart from her and she had missed her that day, although she would have to get used to being without her. She was due to return to work in a couple of weeks' time now that her maternity leave was coming to an end and Beatrix would be looked after by Alison. While Beth knew the other woman would take good care of her, it would be a wrench to leave her. Still, it was what she had to do if she was to provide for her daughter. Maybe Beatrix was destined to have only one parent but Beth didn't intend that she would miss out, financially *or* emotionally.

Her mouth thinned as she lifted Beatrix out of the bath and wrapped her in a towel. One loving parent was more than enough and far better than having someone unreliable in her life like Callum!

The pub served food so Callum had something to eat then went back up to his room. He had spent almost thirty-six hours on the go and he was bone-tired. He desperately needed to sleep and lay down on the bed, fully clothed, but he couldn't settle. He kept thinking about what had happened with Beth and knew that he wouldn't be able to rest until he had resolved at least some of the issues with her.

In the end, he got up and left the pub, taking his time as he walked to the cottage. He had no idea what he was going to say to her when he got there but he needed to convince Beth that he had been telling the truth about her letter failing to reach him for so long. At least, it would be a start if he could do that, a small step towards convincing her about all the rest. Despite what she thought, he *did* care about their daughter. He cared a lot, far more than he would have expected, in fact. He had a child and even though he had never really wanted a family of his own, he intended to do his very best for her…

If only Beth would let him.

The thought felt like a lead weight inside him. Callum was very aware that Beth would have the deciding vote when it came to a decision about his input into their daughter's life. Bearing in mind how she had reacted earlier, it seemed unlikely that she would let him have anything to do with her, and he was devastated at the thought that he might not be able to play any part in his child's life.

He stopped outside the cottage, wondering how best to approach this. He might only get this one chance and he couldn't afford to waste it. Maybe it had hurt to be treated so coldly by Beth before but his feelings didn't matter. It was his daughter who mattered, the child he and Beth had conceived against all the odds that last night.

Callum found his thoughts winging back to that night and he shuddered. He had only gone to see Beth because the papers finalising their divorce had come through that morning. For some reason he still couldn't explain, he had felt that he'd had to acknowledge the ending of their marriage in person. What he had never expected was that they would end up in bed together. He had honestly thought that their desire for one another had died, but that night it had felt just like it had in the beginning. The feel of her hands on his skin, the brush of her lips against his, had transformed their lovemaking into something magical. Special. Something he had never felt before and knew he wouldn't feel again.

His heart ached with a sudden searing pain. He had loved her so much and knew that she had loved him too—how could they have lost sight of that?

Beth tiptoed to the nursery window. Beatrix had fallen asleep and she didn't want to wake her. Reaching up, she went to draw the curtains then paused when she caught sight of Callum standing outside. Her heart leapt even though she'd half expected that he would seek her out again. All of a sudden, she wasn't sure what to do. If she let him in then he would only repeat what he had said earlier and she couldn't see any point in that. He had claimed that it had taken months for her letter to reach him but did she believe him? If he could lie about loving her then he could lie about that too!

Beth felt a wave of anger wash over her as she drew the curtains then made her way downstairs. Opening the front door, she stared, stony-faced, at the man standing outside on the step. He had his hand raised in readiness to knock and she glared at him. 'Beatrix is asleep and I'd appreciate it if you didn't wake her up.'

'Oh. Right.'

He looked momentarily disconcerted, which was rare for him. Callum's confidence was one of the things that had attracted her to him when they had first met. They had both been invited to a mutual friend's birthday party in London, a noisy affair that had grown rowdier as the evening had worn on. Although most of the people there had been similar in age to her, Beth had found their behaviour childish. Their main aim seemed to be to drink as much as they could but getting drunk wasn't something she planned to do.

She was due in work the following day and had no intention of turning up with a hangover, so when one of the men had tried to persuade her to take part in their drinking game, she had refused. The situation had turned ugly then. Beth had felt really frightened when he had grabbed hold of her and forced the glass to her lips, and that's when Callum had stepped in.

He hadn't said a word as he'd removed the glass from the other man's hand and placed it on a table, but his expression had said it all. The man had immediately let her go and hurried away. Only then had Callum spoken and all he'd done was ask her if she was ready to leave. They had left the party and found an all-night café down by the docks. The time had flown past as they had talked about their lives over mugs of tea.

Callum had explained that he worked for an aid agency and that he had only recently returned from India. It was very different from the career path Beth had chosen and she was intrigued to hear more, not that the conversation was in any way one-sided when he'd seemed equally fascinated by what she had done. She had never met anyone who was as easy to talk to as Callum and she'd found herself telling him things she had told no one else. By the time they left the café, she was already half in love with him...

'Look, Beth, I know you said before that you didn't want to hear what I had to say but it's important that we sort this out.'

The urgency in his voice brought her back to the present, although it was hard to rid her mind of the memories. They had been so good together, true soul mates, totally attuned to one another, until she had decided that she wanted them to have a baby. Would their relationship have lasted if she hadn't made that decision? She had no idea. However, it was that thought that made her step back so Callum could come in. If she was even partly responsible for ruining what they'd had then she owed him this at least.

'Come into the sitting room,' she said shortly, leading the way.

Callum followed her in, smiling when he saw the basket of toys tucked under the coffee table. 'I see our daughter's into cars rather than dolls.'

'She loves anything that has wheels.' Beth sat down on the chair, leaving Callum to have the sofa. It would have been too hard to sit next to him and recall all the other times they had sat there, cuddled up together. It was something else she didn't want to dwell on and she sprang to her feet. 'I'll put the kettle on. What d'you want—tea or coffee?'

'Neither, thanks.' He grimaced. 'I drank so much tea and coffee on the journey back here that I'm awash with it.'

'Oh, I see.' Beth hesitated but she really didn't want anything to drink either. It had been more a delaying tactic, but perhaps it would be better to get this over with. The sooner Callum had said his piece, the sooner he would leave and things would get back to normal. It was a relief when he carried on.

'I got here as quickly as I could, Beth. Once I received your letter, I contacted the agency and told them that I needed to return to England immediately.' He shrugged. 'All right, I'll admit that it took a couple of weeks to make the arrangements but there was nothing I could do about that. It was out of my hands.'

He sounded sincere enough and Beth found herself wavering. Was he telling her the truth or was it merely some elaborate tale he had dreamed up to explain his absence? The Callum she had known in the past had never lied to her. Or at least she had *thought* he hadn't done so, she amended swiftly. She didn't want to think that he was lying to her now but how could she trust him after what he had done? He had walked away even though he had claimed to love her. He had even told her that on their last night together, told her that he loved her and that he would always love her. She had taken it to mean that he had changed his mind, that the divorce had been a mistake, and that he wanted them to get back together.

Tears filled her eyes as she recalled how devastated she had felt when she had woken in the morning to find him gone. No, if Callum had truly loved her then he would have *stayed*.

Callum could tell things weren't going well. Beth had tears in her eyes now and he didn't imagine they were tears of joy either. He searched his mind for the right words, words that would convince her he deserved another chance, but in his heart he knew there was nothing he could say to make up for what he had done. He hadn't been here when she had needed him. He hadn't been here for her or their daughter and there was no point explaining how bad he felt about it when she wasn't interested in anything he had to say. Beth didn't want him in her life any more and the pain that thought caused him made him suck in his breath.

He stood up abruptly, his legs trembling so hard that he wasn't sure if they would hold him, but he refused to let her think that he was playing for sympathy.

'I didn't come here to upset you, Beth. It's the last thing I want to do. I've told you the truth but I can see that I was wrong to expect you to believe me.' He spread his hands apart in frustration. 'If there was anything I could do to convince you then I'd do it, but I doubt if you'd be interested even then. I'm no longer part of your life and I accept that, but I hope you will allow me to be part of our daughter's life in some way.' His voice caught then, the words all jammed up inside him as emotion took over, and he stared at the ceiling, not wanting her to guess how agonising it was to know that he might be excluded from his child's future.

'I'll think about it, although I'm not making any promises.'

Beth sounded as choked up as he did and Callum lowered his eyes. His heart scrunched up inside him when he saw the tears that were now trickling down her beautiful face.

'I'm so sorry,' he began, but she held up her hand.

'Don't! I don't want to hear anything else.' She stood up, making it clear that she wanted him to leave.

Callum didn't say another word as he let himself out. He made his way back to the pub, went up to his room, and lay down on the bed, feeling more wretched than he had felt in his entire life.

Even when he had asked Beth for a divorce, he hadn't felt this depth of despair. It had been hard then, heart-wrenchingly hard, but he had been so sure it was the right thing to do. With him out of the way, she would be forced to stop trying to conceive and allow her mind as well as her body to rest. That thought had kept him focused, given him strength. He had loved her *so* much, but he'd had to leave for her sake. Now she didn't want anything to do with him and even though he understood why she felt that way, the thought ripped a hole right through his heart.

CHAPTER THREE

BETH SPENT THE next few days thinking about
what Callum had asked her. The question constantly whizzed around her brain: should she
allow him to have access to Beatrix? Her gut
reaction was to refuse but she knew that she
needed to take her time and think about it. It
wasn't fair to Beatrix to make a snap decision
when it could have such a huge impact on her
life.

When Daniel Saunders, the senior partner at
the practice, phoned to ask her if she would con-
sider returning to work earlier than planned, it
was a relief because it gave her something else
to think about. Apparently, Sandra Nelson, one
of the other GPs, had been rushed into hospital
with appendicitis. With Daniel's wife, Eleanor,

on maternity leave, it meant the practice was currently under a huge amount of pressure.

Beth agreed immediately, even though she hated the thought of leaving Beatrix. She went into the surgery on the Monday morning, realising in surprise that she felt a little bit nervous. Even though she had worked there for a number of years, it felt strange to be back, almost as though she was the new girl. However, she soon got over that feeling when Marie, the receptionist, greeted her in delight.

'Beth!' Marie shot round the desk and enveloped Beth in a hug. 'It's great to have you back. We've missed you!'

'Thank you. I've missed you too,' Beth replied, and realised that she meant it. Although she loved Beatrix to bits, she enjoyed her job and had missed the daily contact with her colleagues and patients. She glanced around the waiting room, smiling when she spotted a couple of early arrivals. 'Not much has changed, I see. The early birds are still here.'

'Too right!' Marie agreed, laughing. 'It's business as usual, although Eleanor's on maternity leave and Bernard has finally retired, though I expect you know that already.'

'I do, but it's nice to be reminded.' Beth rolled her eyes. 'I'm suffering from a bad case of baby brain and keep forgetting things.'

'Don't worry, it will get better, although it could take some time before you're functioning properly,' Marie replied wryly. 'I remember how long it took me to feel halfway normal after I'd had my two.'

'Don't!' Beth laughed. 'You're scaring me to death.' She looked round and smiled when she saw Daniel coming along the corridor. 'Marie was just explaining the pitfalls of motherhood to me.'

'A bit late for that, I'd have thought,' he answered, laughing. He kissed Beth on the cheek. 'Thank you so much for doing this. When Sandra's husband phoned and told me what had happened, I didn't know what we were going to do. I can't tell you how relieved I was when you said you'd come back to work earlier than planned.'

'It isn't a problem,' Beth assured him as they headed to his room. 'I dropped Beatrix off at the childminder's house and I have to say that she didn't appear to be the least bit worried about me leaving her. She was more interested in playing with the other children to miss her mum.'

'Good. It's never easy when you leave them for the first time, whether it's with a childminder or on their first day at school. Why, I even got all choked up when we saw Nathan off to Australia,' he admitted, referring to his nineteen-year-old son who was currently away on his gap year. 'How daft is that?'

'It isn't daft at all,' Beth assured him, smiling. 'Although you'll have to toughen up now that you have Mia. It won't be long before she has a whole load of "firsts" to get through.'

'Don't!' Daniel shuddered at the thought of

going through it all again with his baby daughter. 'Anyway, enough of that. I just wanted to check that you're up to speed. You'll be covering Hemsthwaite Surgery while Sandra's off. I don't think you've worked there before, have you?'

'No. I'd gone on maternity leave when you introduced the new system so that the staff here could take turns working there.'

'I thought so. It's been very useful, I have to say. Although some patients use both surgeries, the majority tend to stick to one or the other. The new system gives everyone a chance to get to know all our patients and that can only be a good thing. Obviously, you'll have access to everyone's notes via the computer so if one of our patients does turn up there, it won't be a problem,' he added.

'It sounds great. I'm looking forward to getting back to work,' Beth explained, truthfully.

'Good. I'm delighted to have you back too. We've been really pushed recently, although

I'm hoping that things are going to improve. If you're agreeable, of course.'

'You want me to do some hours here as well?' Beth queried, wondering why Daniel sounded so grave all of a sudden.

'No, not at all. Covering for Sandra is more than enough at the moment.' He paused and Beth felt her nerves tighten. She was actually holding her breath as she waited for him to continue.

'We desperately need more cover here, though. It was hard enough when there was just Eleanor and me, but now that I'm on my own, it's impossible to keep on top of all the work. I've been trawling the agencies to find a locum but there's nobody suitable willing to work in this part of the world.' He sighed. 'Beautiful countryside can't hold a candle to the bright city lights, it seems.'

'It must be difficult,' she murmured, wondering where this was leading. Daniel rarely prevaricated and that he was doing so now set all her internal alarm bells ringing.

'It is. Which is why I was delighted when I had a phone call from someone I not only know can do the job, but who will also get on with the rest of the team.' He looked her straight in the eyes. 'Callum has asked if he can have a job here, Beth. While I know he's ideal, I don't want to cause any problems for you, so it's your call. What shall I tell him?'

Callum switched off his phone, stunned by what he had just heard. Daniel had called to say that the job was his if he still wanted it. Daniel had been quite blunt when Callum had asked him if there was a vacancy. He had made no bones about the fact that he would need to ask Beth how she felt about Callum working at the surgery. It was the fact that she had agreed that surprised him most of all. Did it mean that she was willing to give him another chance?

He cut that thought dead. There could be a

dozen different reasons why Beth had agreed to him working at The Larches, so he shouldn't go jumping to conclusions. He had spent three wretched days, too wrapped up in his own misery to think clearly. Then, gradually, his mind had started to clear and he had realised what he needed to do. He wasn't going to give up. He was going to find a way to convince Beth that he cared about their daughter. Maybe he would never be able to convince her that he cared about *her* too, but he had to accept that.

Staying in Beesdale was the first step and he couldn't believe his luck when he heard someone mention in the pub one night that the surgery was desperately in need of another doctor. He had phoned Daniel immediately and explained that he was back in Beesdale and looking for a job. Although he hadn't gone into detail, he had also explained about the delay in receiving Beth's letter. It had obviously reassured Daniel to some extent, but he had still added the proviso that he would need to consult Beth before he could take Callum on. And it appeared she hadn't raised any objections. Even though Callum had told himself not to leap to any conclusions, he couldn't help it.

If Beth had hated the idea of him staying in Beesdale then she would never have given the go-ahead for him to work there.

Beth found herself starting to relax once she had seen her first patient. Whether it was the shock of hearing that Callum intended to stay in Beesdale or first-day-back nerves, she had felt incredibly tense when she had arrived at the Hemsthwaite surgery. However, focusing on her patients' problems had soon taken her mind off everything else, even if it was only a temporary reprieve. She buzzed in her next patient, smiling when Diane Applethwaite came into the room. Diane and her husband, Phil, ran a highly successful sheep farm. Their lamb was renowned throughout the Dales for its quality and flavour. With seven children, plus a brand new grandson on the way, Diane was a very busy woman. She was always full of life so Beth was surprised to see how down she looked that day.

'Hello, Diane. Come and sit down.' Beth waited until the other woman was comfortably settled. 'So what can I do for you?'

'I'm not sure what to tell you, Dr Andrews. I just feel so tired all the time, as though I've got no energy left.' Diane sighed. 'It's not like me at all. Phil must be sick of me moping about all over the place. That's why I came to see you.'

'I see. Do you have any other symptoms apart from feeling tired?' Beth asked, mentally running through a list of possible causes. Anaemia was a possibility as a lot of women suffered from that, especially if their monthly periods were heavy. She glanced at Diane's notes and checked her age: forty-eight. It could be the menopause, of course; that could cause a wide range of symptoms from tiredness through to mood swings. Hormone replacement therapy could help if that were the case, although it was too soon to make a diagnosis.

'Not really.' Diane hesitated. 'Although I've felt sick a few times too.'

'Anything else?' Beth prompted when Diane paused again.

'Well, I've not had a period for a while.' She grimaced. 'I used to be regular as clockwork but in the past year, I've been all over the place. Do you think it's the change, Dr Andrews?'

'It's possible, Diane. You're forty-eight and it could very well be the start of the menopause. We'll do some tests, check your hormone levels, and see what they show.'

Diane nodded. 'I thought it might be that. To be honest, I've been dreading it. My mum was terrible when she went through the change, had these awful hot flushes and she was so bad tempered too. I'd hate to think that I'll be like that.'

'There's no reason why you should take after your mother,' Beth said consolingly. 'Every woman is different, plus there's HRT these days, which can help enormously to alleviate the worst symptoms.'

'Is it safe, though? I've read so many conflicting reports about HRT that I'm not sure if I want to take it or not.'

'That's your decision and I certainly wouldn't try to force you to take it,' Beth assured her. 'However, in my opinion, it's extremely safe and very helpful too.' She stood up, not wanting to appear to be pushing Diane into making a decision right then. 'Let's take some blood and see what that shows before we go any further.'

Beth took the sample, deciding it was easier to do it herself rather than ask Diane to wait to see Jane Barton, their practice nurse. Once the tubes were clearly labelled, she popped them into an envelope ready for the courier to collect at lunchtime. 'We should have the results back in a week or so. In the meantime, I'm going to prescribe a course of iron tablets to help with the tiredness. I think you may be a little anae-

mic—the blood results will show if you are—
and the iron will help.'

'Let's hope so. It's a busy time of the year for
us and I could do with a bit more energy. I'll
definitely need it when our Sam and Lauren
have the baby,' Diane declared, sounding much
brighter than when she had arrived.

'It won't be long now,' Beth agreed, thinking how much it could help to talk through a
problem. She sighed inwardly, wondering if she
should have talked to Daniel about the problem she had with Callum before she had agreed
that he could work at The Larches. Maybe it
would have helped a bit, she acknowledged,
but at the end of the day it was something she
had to resolve by herself. She fixed a smile to
her mouth, not wanting to think about her own
worries. 'Are you looking forward to being a
grandmother?'

'That I am. It seems an age since there was a
little one running around the place,' Diane said
with a laugh. 'Steven, my youngest, is seven-

teen now and at least a foot taller than me. He's certainly not a baby any more!'

Beth laughed as she saw Diane out. She worked her way through the rest of the list then went to Reception to wait for the courier. There were several more tests that Jane had collected so she handed them over as well. They closed for lunch but there was an open surgery in the afternoon, plus a visit by the local optician. Hemsthwaite Surgery might be smaller than The Larches and open for fewer hours, but it was still very busy and she would enjoy working there, she decided as she went to lock the door after the courier left.

Her hand was hovering over the catch when she saw a car turn into the car park and she frowned, hoping it wasn't an early arrival. It was only when the driver got out that she realised it was Callum and her heart seemed to skip a beat. What on earth was Callum doing here?

Callum wasn't sure if he should be doing this.

He had intended to give Beth some space but the urge to see her had been too strong to resist. He locked the car then started to walk towards the surgery, his stomach lurching when he saw Beth standing by the door. It was hard to read her expression from this distance but he had the feeling that she wasn't exactly thrilled to see him. It was only the thought of how it would appear if he turned around and went back to the car that kept him walking towards her.

'What are you doing here, Callum?'

There was no welcome in her voice and he sighed under his breath. Obviously, the situation hadn't improved as much as he had hoped it had. Beth was still loath to have anything to do with him and although he could understand it in a way, it was starting to grate on him. His tone was harsher than it might have been, less conciliatory. Beth wasn't the only one who had suffered: he had too.

'I came to thank you for not raising any objections about me being offered the locum post,' he said flatly. 'However, I can see that I'm wasting my time. Jack the Ripper would probably receive a warmer welcome than me!' He swung round, deciding that it would be better if he got back in his car and left. He wasn't helping his case, was he? He was simply putting Beth's back up and that was the last thing he could afford to do.

'Wait!'

Callum slowed, although he didn't stop altogether. Glancing over his shoulder, he saw that Beth had stepped outside and was standing on the path. There was such a look of indecision on her face that he felt his heart suddenly go out to her. That she was torn between sending him packing and talking to him was obvious and he hated to know that he had put her in this position. He didn't want to make life difficult for her but unless they found a way to resolve this situation, it was going to continue to be stressful for both of them. The thought made him turn round and retrace his steps.

'Look, Beth, I didn't come here to start an argument,' he said quietly. 'I simply came to thank you. Daniel told me that I could have the job as long as you didn't raise any objections and I'm just grateful that you agreed.'

'Why? That's what I don't understand, Callum. Why do you want to work here? Why do you want to stay in Beesdale for that matter?'

There was a tremor in her voice that made Callum feel worse than ever. That she was upset was obvious and there was absolutely nothing he could say that would help...apart from telling her the truth, perhaps?

The thought of baring his soul made his stomach clench. Was he prepared to do that, to admit how he felt about becoming a father in the hope that it would convince her to let him see their daughter? What if he said too much? What if the words somehow slipped out and he found himself admitting how he felt about *her*? The thought gave him hot and cold chills because he wasn't sure if he could cope if Beth rejected him.

'Callum…?'

'Have you had lunch yet?' Callum cut her off, knowing that he needed time to work out what he was going to say if he was to avoid a disaster.

'Lunch,' Beth repeated, blankly.

'Mmm. I've got to drive over to Leeds this afternoon to pick up the rest of my stuff from the airport. There wasn't room for it in the plane I flew back on so it had to be sent as freight. I was planning to have lunch on the way so do you fancy joining me?' he said, as though inviting her to have lunch with him was the most natural thing in the world to do. Maybe it should be, he thought suddenly. After all, if they could forge some kind of *normal* relationship then surely it would help?

'I'm not sure it's a good idea,' she said flatly.

'Why not? Look, I know you're angry with me, and I understand why, but I want this to work, Beth. I want to be here for Beatrix, not just now but in the future as well. Maybe I had doubts about becoming a father in the past, but now that it's happened, I know it's what I want.' Callum felt a wave of emotion rise up and almost choke him but he forced himself to carry on. 'The last thing I want is Beatrix growing up, thinking that I don't care about her. I know how destructive that can be, believe me!'

CHAPTER FOUR

BETH SAT ON the old settle and watched as Callum made his way to the bar to order their lunch. It was a beautiful day and the pub was busy with tourists enjoying a day out but she had no problem picking Callum out from the crowd. With his thick dark hair, his tanned skin and that air of authority he exuded, he stood out and she noticed several women glance his way. Callum had always possessed the ability to turn heads, just as he had turned hers when they had first met.

'Right. That's all sorted.' He came back and dropped down beside her.

'What do I owe you?' Beth edged away when she felt his thigh brush against hers. She would have dearly loved to move but every seat was taken and they'd been lucky to find these. She bent down to pick up her bag, steeling herself when her knee accidentally knocked against his. She could feel ripples of sensation running under her skin and bit her lip. She didn't want to feel anything for him, didn't want to be aware of him in any way at all, but it was impossible when even the slightest contact made her skin tingle and her blood heat.

'It's my shout. I invited you, don't forget.'

Callum dismissed her offer to pay her share with a shake of his head. Beth was sorely tempted to argue with him but she decided that it wasn't worth it. She needed to keep things on an even keel and not allow emotions to get in the way. She placed her bag back on the floor, taking care not to touch him this time.

'Have you left Beatrix with the childminder?'

She jumped when he shot the question at her. 'Well, I certainly haven't left her at home on her own,' she replied tartly.

'I didn't think you had,' Callum said quietly.

'I was only asking, Beth. I wasn't having a go at you.'

'No. Of course not. Sorry.' Beth flushed, knowing that she had been far too sharp with her answer. She took a quick breath to calm herself but her nerves were jangling. It wasn't easy being with Callum like this but she had to try to maintain some kind of a balance. 'I left her with Alison Lewis. One of the mums I met at my antenatal classes recommended her and she's very nice—she has a real affinity with the children she minds.'

'I remember her from when I last worked here,' Callum said thoughtfully. 'Doesn't she have twins, a boy and a girl?'

'That's right—Molly and Max. They're three now and Beatrix adores them. She was so excited when I dropped her off this morning because she knew they'd be there to play with.'

'Good. It must make it easier if you know that she's happy,' he observed.

'It does,' Beth agreed, somewhat surprised

by his astuteness. 'I have to admit that it was a wrench to leave her but she didn't seem the least bit worried. She was more interested in playing with the other children than in the fact that Mummy was leaving her!'

'It sounds as though she's got loads of confidence,' Callum said with a smile.

'Oh, she has. She's just like you in that respect.' The words rushed out before she could stop them and she saw an expression of pain cross Callum's face.

'I wish I could see her, Beth. Oh, I know you need time to decide what you intend to do but it would mean such a lot if I could see her.' He stared down at his hands. 'After I received your letter telling me you were pregnant, I spent hours wondering if you'd had a little boy or a little girl. Then ever since I found out she was a girl, I've spent even more time imagining what she looks like.'

He suddenly looked up and Beth felt a lump come to her throat when she saw the yearning in his eyes. 'I mean, is she blonde like you or dark like me? Does she have brown eyes or hazel? At the moment she's just this shadowy little figure who I can't picture clearly and I can't tell you how much it would mean to me to just see her, touch her, *smell* her even. Then I'll really feel that she's my daughter.'

Callum hadn't meant to let his emotions get the better of him. On the contrary, he'd been determined to project a calm front. However, thinking about the daughter he had never seen had let loose a host of feelings, most of which he had never expected to experience. He had never yearned for a child of his own, never longed to procreate even when he and Beth had been trying so hard to have a baby. But now that his daughter was a fact, he found it impossible to take a step back from her.

'Here. I have some photos of her on my phone.'

He jumped when Beth pressed her phone into his hand. He stared at the screen, feeling his emotions multiply a hundredfold as he looked at the fair-haired moppet smiling up at him. She had Beth's colouring and his eyes. She also had his nose if he wasn't mistaken.

Words failed him as he flicked through the photos, one after the other. They were a record of his daughter's life to date, the first one taken straight after her birth and the last one only a couple of days ago. All those months that had passed without him being there, he thought wretchedly. All that time during which she had grown up and he had known nothing about her existence.

How he longed to turn back the clock, to have been there for her from the very first moment, but it was impossible. He could never recapture that precious time he'd lost; all he could do was to make sure that he was there for the rest of her life. The thought stiffened his resolve, made him see just how important this was to him. He wasn't going to give up. Even if Beth refused his pleas then he would find a way to maintain contact with his daughter.

'She's beautiful,' he said, reluctantly relinquishing the phone. 'She has your colouring and my eyes.'

'Yes.' Beth bit her lip and he could sense her hesitation before she hurried on. 'I think she has your nose as well, although babies change so quickly that it's hard to be certain. One minute they look like one parent and the next they look like the other.'

'It must be fascinating, seeing all the changes,' he said, struggling to control the emotions that kept welling up inside him. He cleared his throat when he saw Beth glance at him, not sure if he felt comfortable about laying himself bare this way. It would have been different if they'd still been together; he wouldn't have felt nearly as self-conscious then. But they were no longer together, no longer involved apart from through their child, and he needed to protect himself.

'It is. Every day Beatrix seems to change. It's not just how she looks either but what she can do.' She smiled, her beautiful face lighting up with delight. 'I swear she said "dog" the other day when I took her out for a walk.'

'Sure it was "dog"?' Callum asked, adopting a deliberately sceptical tone because he couldn't afford to think about how much he wanted her at that moment.

'Well, I'm not sure exactly, but it sounded very much like it,' she said defensively.

Callum laughed. 'I'll take your word for it. After all, you know her better than anyone else does.'

'I do.' She took a quick breath and he steeled himself for what he was about to hear. 'It's been just Beatrix and me right from the very beginning, Callum, and that's how I want it to continue.'

'Meaning there's no place for me?' he said harshly as his worst fears coalesced into one terrible thought: Beth was going to refuse to let him see his daughter. She wasn't going to allow him to have any contact with her. Oh, maybe he could go through the courts and apply for visitation rights, but how would that help? Beth would only resent him if she was forced to grant him access and Beatrix would soon realise there was something wrong. Could he do that to her, could he put his child through that kind of trauma, make her suffer at the hands of two warring parents? Of course not!

'Why do you want to play a part in her life, anyway?'

Beth answered his question with a question of her own and Callum drew himself up short. Was it a sign that she hadn't completely made up her mind about this? That she was willing to reconsider if he could prove his case? The thought made his insides churn with nerves but if there was one occasion when he needed to appear confident, it was now.

'Because I know how important it is, not just for me but, more crucially, for Beatrix.' He had never told Beth about his unhappy childhood. Whenever the subject had come up, he had brushed it aside. However, now it was time to tell her the whole story. His tone was flat when he continued because he had long since come to terms with the past and it no longer had the power to affect him.

'My parents never really wanted me, you see. They're both lawyers and run their own firm, specialising in international property rights. They spend a lot of time flying to one place or another, so my arrival was merely a hindrance. I spent my early years being looked after by a succession of nannies then, once I was old enough, I was sent away to school.'

'How old were you then?'

Callum heard the shock in her voice but he didn't dwell on it. His past no longer mattered apart from if it helped to make his case to see his daughter. 'Seven.'

'So young!' she exclaimed.

He shrugged. 'Most of the boys were the same age as me when they started at the school, so it was quite normal.'

'Did you miss them, your parents, I mean?'

she queried, obviously finding it difficult to understand.

'Not really. I'd had very little to do with them so it really didn't worry me. In fact, it was holidays that were the worst times. It was obvious that they resented spending time with me when they could have been working. In fact, it was a relief when I was old enough to go away on holiday on my own and do various activities like skiing or diving.'

'I can't imagine what it must have been like,' she admitted. 'My family has always been close and we enjoyed spending time together.'

'You were lucky.' Callum smiled at her. 'Not everyone has such a good relationship with their parents.'

'So it seems,' Beth replied, her voice wobbling. 'Do you see much of them nowadays?'

'No.' Callum could tell that she fighting back tears and felt dreadful about it but he couldn't afford to weaken if he was to plead his case. 'We go our separate ways and that suits us fine.

However, there's no denying that my childhood had an effect on me. That's why I was so reluctant when you suggested we should have a baby. I was afraid that I'd turn out like them and not really be interested in my child, but I was wrong.'

He held her gaze, knowing that this was the most important moment of his life. He had to convince her that he meant every word. 'As soon as I learned that we had a child, everything changed. Maybe I don't know how to be a proper father yet but I'll learn—I promise you that. Just give me a chance, Beth. Give *Beatrix* a chance to get to know me because I swear on my life that I'll never let her down.'

Beth collected Beatrix from Alison's house and drove home. The afternoon had passed in a blur. Callum's revelation about his childhood had answered so many questions she had wondered about but he'd never wanted to talk about it before. How awful it must have been for him to feel unwanted! Coming from a loving home herself, it was hard to understand how anyone could behave that way towards their own child, but she knew that he had been telling her the truth.

He hadn't made up some sob story to persuade her to let him see their daughter; every heartbreaking word had been true. She couldn't begin to explain how much it hurt to know how he must have suffered.

She let them into the cottage and set Beatrix on the sitting room floor so she could play with her toys while Beth made her tea. She boiled an egg and made toast soldiers to go with it then fetched Beatrix through to the kitchen and popped her in the highchair. The little girl was at the messy stage of wanting to feed herself but it was all part and parcel of growing up.

Beth helped her spoon some egg into her mouth then handed her a finger of toast. Some of it ended up in Beatrix's hair, which she seemed to think was the perfect spot for wiping her hands, but Beth didn't mind. Beatrix was happy and healthy and loved and they were the things that mattered most.

Tears suddenly welled to her eyes again as she thought about Callum and what he had told her, *how* he had told her. There'd been no sadness in his voice, no anger, no pain. It made her see just how awful it must have been for him to live through a childhood like that. No wonder he was so determined to be there for their daughter.

Standing up, Beth went into the sitting room and found her phone. Maybe she wasn't one hundred per cent certain that she was doing the right thing but she knew that she would never forgive herself if at some point in the future Beatrix thought that her father hadn't wanted anything to do with her. She bit her lip as she pressed the dial button. She didn't want to add to Callum's pain either.

Callum had just taken a shower when his phone rang. Digging through the pile of clothes on the bed, he finally unearthed it, his heart racing when he saw Beth's name appear on the screen. He still wasn't sure if he had done the right thing by telling her about his childhood. What if it had simply confirmed her fears that he wasn't fit to be Beatrix's father? By his own admission he knew nothing about being a parent and he couldn't blame her if she had decided to cut him out of their daughter's life.

'Hello,' he said, hoping she couldn't tell how nervous he felt.

'I was wondering if you were busy this evening,' she said quietly, although he heard the tremor in her voice that she was trying to disguise.

'Not unless you call going down to the bar to sample yet more pub grub busy,' he replied with forced levity. 'I'm not exactly fussy when it comes to food but if I have to eat another pie then I might just keel over!'

'Oh, dear.' She laughed and Callum felt his

spirits lift. Beth had the most wonderful laugh, warm and genuine, just like her.

'Well, I can't promise cordon bleu cooking but I can rustle something up for us and it won't be a pie, I promise you.' She took a quick breath and then hurried on. 'I thought you might like to come round and meet Beatrix.'

Beth opened the sitting room door but Callum didn't move. She glanced at him, feeling her heart ache when she saw the expression on his face. Beatrix had already had her bath and she was wearing her favourite pyjamas, the ones printed with pink bunny rabbits. She looked so adorable as she sat on the rug playing with a toy car that Beth's own heart melted. It wasn't hard to understand how Callum must feel at that moment, just how overwhelming it must be for him.

Without pausing to think, she took hold of his hand and led him into the room. His fingers were icy-cold and her emotions see-sawed once more. She had intended to keep this first meeting low-key but it was impossible to pretend that it wasn't of major importance for both him and Beatrix. For if it was the first time that Callum had seen his daughter then it was the first time that Beatrix had seen her father too. Tears stung her eyes at the thought but she blinked them away. Letting go of Callum's hand, she went over and knelt down on the rug beside Beatrix.

'There's someone here to see you, darling,' she said softly. 'Say hello.'

Beatrix looked up, her big brown eyes fastening on the stranger standing by the door. Just for a moment her lower lip wobbled ominously before Callum stepped forward. Crouching down, he picked up a car and ran it across the rug.

'Broom, broom. Beep, beep,' he said as he steered it towards the little girl.

Beatrix's face broke into a huge smile as she took the car from him and pushed it across the rug, making appropriate beeping noises. Callum laughed. 'She's obviously going to be a racing driver when she grows up.'

'Looks like it.' Beth felt a wave of relief wash over her. There'd been a moment when she had thought that Beatrix might get upset at seeing a stranger in their home but, somehow, Callum had immediately struck the right note with her. Was it a sign that it would be easier than she had feared to let him into their lives? She sighed softly. It was too soon to speculate about that. Far too soon either to know if his interest would last.

The doubts rushed in before she could stop them and she scrambled to her feet, not wanting to go down that route at this moment. There would be time for that later, time when she would have to weigh up the pros and the cons of this situation, although there could be only one outcome. Beatrix's happiness came first and if she had any concerns at all about her precious daughter then she would call a halt, even if it meant disappointing Callum.

'I've done salmon and new potatoes for us. I hope that's all right. It's just about ready so I suggest we eat while madam here is happily engaged with her cars.'

Her tone was overly bright and she saw Callum shoot an assessing look at her. He didn't say anything, however; he simply ran his hand over Beatrix's hair as he stood up, and the very simplicity of the gesture moved Beth more than she could say.

It was obvious that he wanted this to work, but was wanting enough? It wasn't easy being a parent. He'd need to make some massive changes to his life and she wasn't sure if he understood that. After all, he had very little experience of what it took to be a father after the less than ideal childhood he'd had. It was a worrying thought and Beth's mind was racing as she served their meal. Callum sighed as he took his first bite.

'This is delicious. You shouldn't have gone to so much trouble, although I'm glad that you did. My arteries will be able to have a day off from all that grease.'

'Eating out is fine but not when you have to do it every day,' she agreed, finding it easier to stick to a more neutral topic. Maybe they both needed to take a step back from all the heavy emotional stuff, she mused. It had been full-on ever since Callum had reappeared and it might help if they found some kind of balance so she carried on in the same vein. 'Are you going to continue staying at the pub or do you plan to find somewhere else to live while you're covering for Eleanor's maternity leave?'

'I'm going to move into the flat over the surgery. Daniel asked me if I'd like to move in there and I jumped at the chance.' He speared a piece of fish then looked at her. 'It will give me time to look around for somewhere permanent.'

'Permanent?' Beth echoed, unable to hide her surprise. 'You mean that you intend to *stay* in Beesdale?'

'Of course.'

'But what about your aid work?' she asked, her heart racing. Callum was planning to live here permanently—could it be true? He had lived here once before, of course, when he had first moved to Yorkshire to be with her. Although he had never said so at the time, she'd had the impression that he hadn't really settled into the role of country GP. The thought set all her internal alarm bells clanging and she hurried on. 'I know how much you enjoy the work you do, so are you sure you'll be happy switching careers?'

'Yes. Oh, don't get me wrong, I love my job, but my priorities have changed. I have a child now and there's no way that I intend to go trekking off around the globe when she needs me.'

There! He'd said it, actually put into words all the vague ideas he'd had since he had returned to England. He intended to be here for Beatrix, not just for a few months, either, but permanently. He wanted to watch her growing up and have some real input into her life. He had no idea how Beth would feel about the idea, but he would worry about that later. For now it was enough to make his position clear.

'I don't know what to say, Callum. When you turned up, I thought it was just going to be… well, a brief visit.'

'So did I at first. Oh, not too brief. I did plan to stay around to sort things out—' He broke off. Admitting that he had hoped to sort things out with her seemed like a pipe dream now. It was obvious that she didn't want him back and, although it upset him terribly, he had to accept it. He would be Beatrix's father—no more and certainly no less than that. If Beth would let him.

The thought that even now she might not allow him to have any contact with his daughter in the future sent a rush of panic shooting through him. He pushed away his plate, all thoughts of food forgotten. 'I know it very much depends on you, Beth, but I hope you'll believe me when

I say that I'm serious about this. I want to be a real father to Beatrix.'

'But for how long, though?'

The scepticism in her voice cut close to the bone but he didn't dare show it. He couldn't afford to let her see that he had his own doubts about his ability to live up to the role. 'For ever. There's no time limit on being a parent as far as I'm aware.'

'No, there isn't. It's a lifetime commitment, Callum—are you really prepared for that?' She gave a brittle laugh. 'You don't exactly have a good track record when it comes to commitment, do you?'

'Meaning when we split up?' He sighed, wishing he could explain why he'd had to leave her. Should he tell her the truth, that it had been just too painful to watch her torturing herself, that he'd hoped she would find some kind of balance if he was no longer around? He had left because he had loved her, but how could he tell her that when it was unlikely she'd want to hear it? The last thing he wanted was for it to lead to another destructive argument. 'That was different, Beth.'

'Was it? Really? You got tired of me and left, so who's to say you won't get tired of being Beatrix's father and decide to leave her too?'

'I won't. I swear on my life that it won't happen,' he said hotly, hating the fact that she had such a poor opinion of him. 'She's my daughter and I'll never abandon her!'

'You say that now, Callum, but I'm not totally convinced.'

It was obvious that she wasn't prepared to give an inch and he sighed in frustration. 'Then I'll have to prove that I mean it. That's all I'm asking for, Beth, a chance to prove to you that I can be a proper father to our daughter. Oh, I don't expect to jump straight in and become a major part of her life. She needs time to get to know me first. But I want to be involved, take her to the park, teach her how to ride a bike—do all the things that fathers do.'

'And what about the other times, like when she's sick or just being a typical toddler and throwing a tantrum? Will you still want to be her father then?'

'Yes, I will,' he said firmly. Maybe he did have doubts about his ability to take on the role but he wouldn't fail through lack of effort. He intended to put his heart and his soul into making a success of this. If Beth would let him. He stared down at his hands, willing himself to say the words even though they hurt so much.

'I know it didn't work out for us, Beth, but that's all in the past. You'll meet someone else one day and put it behind you. It's the future that matters now, your future, my future but, more importantly, Beatrix's future.' He looked up, trying to hide his devastation at the thought of Beth loving anyone else. 'And I intend to be part of her future.'

CHAPTER FIVE

'SO WHAT'S HAPPENED? Have you seen Callum again?'

'Yes. He's coming round tonight, in fact.' Beth unfastened the sphygmomanometer cuff and rolled it up. Now that Polly was pregnant, she had offered to do her friend's antenatal check-ups. She noted down the blood pressure reading then smiled at her. 'Close your mouth. You look like a goldfish, gaping at me like that.'

'Is it any wonder?' Polly grumbled, rolling down her sleeve. She fixed Beth with a piercing stare. 'I've only been away for two weeks on my honeymoon and look what's happened. You and Callum are getting all cosy again!'

'That's where you're wrong.' Beth got up and took the sample of urine over to the workbench to test it for sugar. Peeling off one of the chemically coated strips, she dipped it into the pot. 'Callum is coming to see Beatrix, not me.'

'If you expect me to believe that,' Polly began, but Beth didn't let her finish.

'Well, you'll have to believe it. He isn't interested in me. He's only interested in his daughter.' She tossed the test strip into the bin then sat down again. 'Everything's fine—blood pressure, sugar level all normal.'

'That's good,' Polly said distractedly. She leant across the desk, her pretty face filled with concern. 'Are you sure he's telling you the truth, Beth? I mean, I wouldn't be at all surprised if he was feeding you a line because he can't bring himself to admit that he's still crazy about you. After all, he came back, didn't he? That has to prove something.'

'He came back to see Beatrix,' Beth corrected her. 'It didn't have anything to do with me. If he hadn't found out that we had a child then he wouldn't have bothered, believe me.'

'It's so sad. I always thought you two would make a go of it eventually,' Polly declared. 'Oh, I know how awful it must have been for you when Callum didn't reply to your letter, but now you know what happened, are you sure there isn't any chance of you getting back together?'

'No. The only reason Callum would want us to get back together is if he thought it would benefit Beatrix,' Beth said baldly. 'He isn't interested in us having a relationship again and neither am I.'

'I see.' Polly sighed as she stood up. 'Well, you know best, Beth, but I still think it's a crying shame if you two don't try to work things out. You went through such a lot together and I find it hard to believe that you don't still have feelings for one another.'

'I'm not saying that,' Beth said quietly, feeling a lump come to her throat. It was difficult to admit that she still cared about Callum when he obviously didn't feel anything for her any more. She held up her hand when Polly went to speak. 'I do care about him but he's made it very clear that what we had is over. He even mentioned me meeting someone else.'

'Maybe you should,' Polly conceded. 'After all, if you and Callum really are history then it's time you moved on. You can't live in the past for ever, Beth.'

Beth sighed after Polly left. She knew that her friend meant well but the thought of meeting anyone else held very little appeal after what had happened between her and Callum. She had thought that they would be together for ever, that their love could overcome any obstacle, but she had been so very wrong. Did she really want to risk going through that kind of heartache again? Of course not!

'Right, Mr Brimsdale, you can put your shirt back on.'

Callum helped the old man into his shirt then went and sat down behind the desk. Arnold Brimsdale was his first patient that morning.

At over ninety years of age, Arnold had come into the surgery for his six-monthly check-up. Now Callum smiled as the old man came to join him. 'Well, I have to say that I wish more of our patients were in as good health as you are, Mr Brimsdale. Your blood pressure is spot on and you've got a good strong heartbeat. The only thing slightly amiss is your breathing but so long as you keep using your inhaler, it shouldn't cause a problem.'

'That's good to hear, Doctor.' Arnold sat down in front of the desk and laughed. 'I'm hoping to get my telegram from the Queen before I pop me clogs. It'll look right nice on the mantel-piece, it will.'

'It will indeed!' Callum laughed as well. He had forgotten how much he enjoyed the Dales people's dry sense of humour. He filled in a repeat prescription for Arnold's inhalers and emailed it to the on-site pharmacy. 'Unless you have any problems I'll see you in six months' time. Don't forget to collect your prescription on your way out, will you?'

'I won't,' Arnold assured him, standing up. 'I take it that you're staying around here then from what you just said.'

'Yes. I'm covering for Dr Saunders while she's on maternity leave, but I'm hoping to be taken on permanently after that,' Callum explained, thinking about the conversation he'd had that morning with Daniel. Although Daniel hadn't actually offered him a permanent post, it was definitely on the cards and now he just needed to tell Beth. The thought of how she would react to the news made his stomach churn but he managed to hide his unease. 'The practice could do with another doctor now that Dr Hargreaves has retired.'

'Aye, that it could, plus that little lass of yours needs her daddy,' Arnold observed before he took his leave.

Callum sighed as the door closed. Everyone in Beesdale knew he was Beatrix's father and they were probably waiting to see if he measured up to the job too. He hadn't exactly got off to a flying start but, hopefully, they wouldn't hold it against him. At least his colleagues at the surgery knew about Beth's letter failing to reach him. It could have been very awkward if they'd all thought he had deserted her when she had needed him most. He would never have left if he'd thought there was a chance of her getting pregnant, though. He would have stayed right here and they could have looked forward to the birth of their baby together. How different his life would have been then.

He blanked out that thought because it was pointless thinking like that. He'd done what he had thought was right at the time, and now he had to live with the consequences. Would Beth follow his advice and move on? he wondered suddenly. Part of him hoped that she would while another part rebelled at the thought of her meeting someone else. He sighed as he buzzed in his next patient. If some passing genie could grant him a wish then it would be to have Beth back in his life, Beth *and* Beatrix, but genies were few and far between in the Yorkshire Dales!

Beth just had time to tidy up before Callum arrived that evening. They had slipped into a routine whereby he called round after work and spent an hour or so playing with Beatrix. She hadn't invited him to dinner again, however; it had seemed wiser to keep things on a less familiar footing. After all, Callum wasn't coming to see her, he was coming to see their daughter, and there was no reason to turn his visits into anything more than they actually were.

Beatrix was delighted to see him each day and held up her arms to be picked up. She had accepted his presence in her life with an ease that Beth envied. Now she sighed as she picked up a pile of clean baby clothes and took them up to the nursery. Even though she knew how silly it was, she was always on edge when Callum was there.

Oh, he never said anything to alarm her. On the contrary, he always confined their conversations to what Beatrix had done. However, just having him in the house made Beth feel very self-conscious. She couldn't help remembering when they had lived there together and how different it had been. Even though their relationship had been under a lot of strain, there had been good times too. Lots of them.

She pushed that thought aside, not wanting to dwell on it. Leaving the clothes on the changing table, she ran back downstairs, forcing a smile when she found Callum playing a game of peek-a-boo with their daughter. Beatrix was giggling in delight, loving every second of it too. 'It looks like you two are having fun,' she observed as she went to join them.

'We are.' Callum covered his face with his hands then peeped through his fingers. 'Peek-a-boo!'

Beatrix laughed so hard that she tumbled over. Beth quickly righted her, placing a steadying hand under her arm as she scrambled to her feet. 'She managed to walk all the way to the chair on her own this morning,' she told Callum as Beatrix shuffled her way to the basket of toys.

'Really?' Callum sounded impressed. 'Some babies don't even attempt to walk until they're much older, do they?'

'No, apparently not,' Beth agreed. 'Obviously, Beatrix is keen to explore the big wide world.'

'It must be in her genes,' Callum replied, laughing. 'I was always eager to see something of the world.'

'Yet you ended up here in the Dales,' Beth said flatly. She sighed but there was no way that she could let the comment pass unchallenged. 'Are you sure you know what you're doing, Callum? Moving here to live is going to be a huge change for you.'

'I've lived here before,' he pointed out.

'Yes, and it wasn't exactly a roaring success,

was it?' she shot back as all her doubts came flooding back. She had tried her best to ignore them but it was impossible. At the back of her mind the thought that Callum would eventually grow tired of living in the town nagged away at her. Beatrix would grow to love him and then he would suddenly disappear from her life.

'I'm not sure I understand what you mean,' he said flatly. 'I certainly didn't have any complaints about my work at the surgery. In fact, Daniel has made it clear that he's more than willing to offer me a permanent post once Eleanor's maternity leave has finished.'

It made perfect sense. Daniel would be keen to offer Callum a post at the surgery because he knew that Callum could do the job and that he fitted in. However, it wasn't that which worried her. 'I wasn't talking about whether or not you can do the job, Callum. That isn't an issue.'

'Then what's the problem?'

'The problem is whether you'll grow tired of being tied to one place. I got the feeling that you found it rather restricting working here the last time.'

'Did I ever say so?' His tone was hard and she sighed. She didn't want to start an argument but he needed to take a good hard look at what he was planning.

'No, you didn't, but I could sense how you felt, tell that you were getting fed up with being in one place all the time.' She shrugged. 'I'm sure it was a contributing factor as to why you left. You'd not only had enough of me but you'd had enough of living here as well.'

Callum wanted to refute what she was saying but how could he? The reason he had left Beesdale—left her!—had nothing whatsoever to do with him growing bored with country life. He had got over his desire to move around all the time by then, worked the wanderlust out of his system. However, if he told Beth that then he would have to tell her the truth, that he had left because watching the woman he loved putting herself through such torment month after month had been unbearable.

'People change,' he said neutrally.

'Do they?' She shrugged. 'I've never really believed that, I'm afraid. You are who you are and that's it.'

'Meaning that I'm never going to settle down and one day I'll decide I've had enough and pack my bags and leave again?' He shook his head, wishing that he could make her understand how wrong she was. 'It's not going to happen, Beth. Especially now.' He looked pointedly at Beatrix.

'So you're going to stay purely for Beatrix's sake?'

'Yes,' he said curtly, hating the fact that she didn't believe him. What made it worse was the fact that he knew it was his fault too. He had left her, so she was bound to have doubts.

'And how long will it be before you come to resent it, resent *Beatrix* because you feel that you have to stay for her sake?' She shook her head, the soft blonde curls dancing around her face. 'Don't say it won't happen, Callum, because I know that it will.'

'You know no such thing!' he exploded because it hurt to know what she thought about him. He leant forward, feeling his senses whirl as he inhaled the scent of her shampoo and was suddenly transported back in time. The familiar fragrance unleashed a flood of memories as he recalled all the other times he had smelled it when Beth had stepped out of the shower each morning and into his arms...

'Just because I left you, Beth, it doesn't mean that I'll leave our daughter,' he said harshly, needing to rid his mind of such dangerous thoughts. 'I love her and I'll always be here for her.'

She drew back abruptly and he frowned when he saw the pain in her eyes. 'Then let's hope you mean what you say this time, Callum. Now I think it's time you left. I have to be in work early tomorrow for the team meeting and I need to put Beatrix to bed.'

Callum wasn't sure what he'd said, although it was obvious that he had upset her. However, short of trying to prise it out of her, there was little he could do. He said his goodbyes and left, taking his time as he walked back to the surgery. He headed straight round to the back where there were steps leading to the flat above. He had moved in the previous week and was slowly settling in. Fortunately, the flat was fully furnished so he hadn't needed to worry about furniture, although he would have to do so when he bought a place of his own.

He sighed. He had moved around such a lot that he had never collected many belongings. When he and Beth had got married she had been amazed to find how little he owned apart from some personal items—clothing and books, that kind of thing. However, if he bought a house then he would have to furnish it and make it comfortable for Beatrix when she came to stay with him—*if* she came to stay with him, he amended swiftly.

He frowned. What on earth had he said to upset Beth so much?

Beth arrived at the surgery the following morning just as Daniel was unlocking the doors. He waved to her then went inside to switch off the alarm. Beth took a deep breath as she got out of her car. She'd hardly slept and she felt tired and drained. Although she knew how stupid it was to have let it affect her, that comment of Callum's had really thrown her. He couldn't have made it any plainer if he had spelled it out for her that he had never really loved her at all. It made her wonder if everything she'd thought they'd had together had been a sham. The idea that she had been fooling herself about how Callum had felt about her was excruciating, but she had to face up to it. She may have loved him with every fibre of her being but it appeared that he had never felt the same way about her.

Daniel had the kettle on by the time Beth made her way inside. He looked round and grimaced. 'Mia had us up all night so I'm in need of a strong dose of caffeine to get me going.'

'Me too,' Beth agreed fervently, earning herself a quizzical look. 'It was one of those nights when you just can't seem to settle,' she explained hastily, not wanting to go into the whys and wherefores of why she'd been awake. 'What was wrong with Mia anyway? I saw Eleanor at the shops the other day and she told me that Mia was sleeping through the night now.'

'Normally, she does, but she had a touch of colic and we couldn't get her settled.' Daniel spooned coffee into the machine and switched it on. 'Needless to say, she was fast asleep this morning when Eleanor and I had to get up.'

'Typical!' Beth drummed up a laugh, hoping it didn't sound as forced to Daniel as it did to her. She looked round when she heard footsteps coming along the corridor and felt her heart jolt when Callum appeared.

'Ah, coffee. Great stuff,' he declared, coming into the kitchen. He nodded to Beth then turned to Daniel and started to tell him about a call he had made the previous day.

Beth frowned. Although she had been upset when Callum had left her house last night, she was sure that she had hidden it. However, there was no denying that there seemed to be a definite atmosphere all of a sudden. Despite the way he was regaling Daniel with the tale of what had gone on, Callum looked uneasy and it wasn't like him. Beth chewed it over but she was no closer to finding an explanation by the time the rest of the team arrived. Once everyone had a drink they adjourned to the meeting room. Beth found herself sitting next to Owen Walsh, who had recently taken over the running of the on-site pharmacy. He smiled when she sat down beside him.

'Hi, you must be Beth. It's nice to meet you at last.'

'And you too,' she replied, taking an immediate liking to his open and friendly manner. 'How are you settling in?'

'Fine. Everyone's been very welcoming, I'm relieved to say.' He grinned at her. 'I was a bit worried in case people saw me as an incomer and were a bit sniffy about me taking the job, but they've been great.'

'Beesdale is a really friendly little town,' she assured him. 'I found everyone very welcoming when I moved here. The only downside is that the locals love to know everything about you, so if you have any skeletons in your cupboards then be warned. They will find out!'

'Thanks for the advice.' Owen laughed. 'I'll make sure I fit some strong locks to my cupboards.'

Daniel called the meeting to order then so Beth turned her attention to what was being said. There was always a lot to get through and there was no time to waste. Marie was having problems with the computer and Daniel asked her to phone the IT specialists so they could check it out as it was vital to the smooth running of the surgery.

Beth's gaze moved on around the rest of the group, coming to a halt on Callum, who was sitting off to her right, and she felt her breath catch when she realised that he was watching her. Just for a moment their eyes met before he looked away but she could feel her heart racing. What had she seen in his eyes? For a second it had looked almost like pain but that couldn't be right. Callum didn't care about her; he never really had cared. Yet no matter how many times she told herself that, it was hard to believe it.

Callum couldn't believe the agony he felt as he watched Beth laughing with Owen Walsh. He clenched his hands, forcing down the pain. He knew he should be glad that she looked so happy as she sat there, listening to what Walsh was saying, but it was impossible. He didn't want to see her enjoying some other man's company. He wanted her to enjoy his! And it was pure unmitigated torture to have to sit there and pretend that he didn't care. When Daniel asked him a question, it took a tremendous effort just to string together an answer.

The meeting came to an end at last and Callum made his escape. He went straight to his room and brought up his morning list on the computer, sighing in frustration when halfway through the screen went blank. Leaving his desk, he went through to Reception where Marie was struggling to get the system working again.

'It's no good,' she declared, turning to him. 'I can't get it going. I'll have to phone the IT guy to see if he can sort it out. In the meantime, we'll have to go back to the old system of giving everyone a number when they arrive.'

'Can we still access their notes?' Callum

asked, glancing over his shoulder when he heard voices in the corridor.

'I doubt it,' Marie admitted. 'The whole system seems to have gone down. I'll have to dig out everyone's paper file, although I'm not sure how up to date they are.'

'What's happened?'

Callum steeled himself when he heard Beth's voice. It took every scrap of willpower he could muster to turn and face her. 'The computer's packed up completely now so Marie's going to get straight on to the IT guy. In the meantime, we'll have to use the paper files to check the patients' notes.'

'I'd better check the pharmacy computer,' Owen Walsh declared anxiously. He touched Beth's arm. 'I'll give you a call at the weekend, if that's all right?'

'Yes. Fine. I'll look forward to it,' Beth replied, smiling at him.

Callum counted to ten but he still couldn't manage to hold back the question that was clamouring to get out. 'Why is Walsh going to phone you?'

'To make arrangements for us to go out for dinner some time,' Beth replied coolly. 'Although I really don't see what business it is of yours, Callum.'

'It's my business if it impacts on Beatrix,' he said harshly.

'I think it's up to me to worry about that, don't you?' She turned to Marie, ignoring him as she asked the receptionist's advice if any patients from the Larches turned up at the Hemsthwaite surgery and she couldn't access their notes.

Callum went back to his room, his temper soaring. Why, for two pins he would ban Beth from going out with Walsh, he thought furiously, then sighed when he realised how ridiculous it was to think he could do that. He had no control over what Beth did or with whom she did it either and the thought cut right through him. The idea of her meeting someone else might have been fine in theory, but the reality was very different. He took a deep breath, knowing that he had to rein in his emotions. If he didn't do so then Beth might decide to cut him out of her life altogether and he would never see her or Beatrix again.

CHAPTER SIX

BETH WAS GLAD to see a long queue when she arrived at the Hemsthwaite surgery. She needed to keep busy in the hope that it would take her mind off the strange way Callum had behaved that morning. Mandy Stephens, their reception-ist, had been alerted to the problems with the computer and was busily hunting out paper files for those patients who had turned up. She gri-maced when Beth went into the surgery.

'I'm not sure how up to date these are now ev-erything's done on the computer,' she explained anxiously, blowing the dust off a couple of buff-coloured folders.

'We'll just have to do the best we can and hope the IT chap can sort out the problem,' Beth told her, deliberately downplaying any problems they might encounter when she saw how flustered Mandy looked. She glanced around the waiting room, smiling when she spotted Diane Applethwaite. At least Diane's test results should be available as the lab they used always sent through a printed report rather than rely solely on email.

'I suppose so.' Mandy handed her the folders. 'They're in order and I've given everyone a number so they know who's next.'

'Thanks. That's really helpful,' Beth declared, smiling at her. Leaving Mandy to carry on finding files, she went to her room and got settled in. Just for a moment her mind flicked back to Callum's reaction about Owen asking her out. He had sounded decidedly put out about it but why? He'd been the one to raise the subject of her meeting someone else, so why should he care if she went out with Owen? It was a mystery, although she didn't intend to dwell on it. She and Callum were divorced and it was none of his business what she did.

The morning flew past with very few problems, thankfully enough. Most people had come with new complaints rather than long-standing conditions that would have required an in-depth study of their case histories. Beth asked anyone she wanted to double-check on to make an appointment on their way out and was confident that she hadn't overlooked anything vital. By the time Diane Applethwaite came into the consulting room, she was feeling far more relaxed and smiled at her.

'Sorry about the wait but the computer's packed up so we're having to go back to the old-fashioned way of doing things. I hadn't realised how much extra time it took.'

'Computers are great when they work but a real pain when they have a hissy fit,' Diane agreed, sitting down. 'Phil has a real love-hate relationship with ours. I've had to rescue it a couple of times from the barn after it's failed to give up some vital bit of information. Mind you, I think it's more Phil's fault than the machine's. He's not what you'd call technologically minded.'

Beth laughed. 'Oh, dear. It's a good job you're there to sort things out. Right, let's have a look at those test results and see what they say.' She took the printed sheet out of Diane's file and scanned through it then read it a second time, more slowly.

'What's wrong, Dr Andrews? I can tell from your expression that something's happened,' Diane said worriedly.

'There's nothing wrong. But the results aren't exactly what I thought they would be.' Beth put the sheet on the desk and looked at Diane, wondering how to break the news to her. However, there really was only one way. 'Far from being in the early stages of the menopause, Diane, it appears that you're pregnant.'

'Pregnant?' Diane repeated, sounding shocked. 'But I'm forty-eight. How can I be pregnant at my age?'

'It's unusual, yes, but it isn't unheard of,' Beth

said gently. 'There have been cases of women becoming pregnant well into their fifties, in fact.'

'I don't know what to say... ' Diane broke off and gulped.

'It must be a lot to take in,' Beth said, sympathetically. 'Maybe you should speak to your husband before you decide what you want to do.'

'What I want to do... What do you mean?' Diane asked in confusion.

Beth chose her words with care. 'In case you decide not to go ahead with the pregnancy.'

'Oh, no. I couldn't do that,' Diane declared. She took a deep breath. 'If it's right and I am having a baby then I'll just have to get on with it.' She suddenly laughed. 'Although what Phil's going to say about us having another little one keeping us awake at night, I have no idea!'

Beth laughed too, delighted that Diane had taken the news so well. 'I'm sure he'll cope brilliantly, the same as you will. After all, you've had a lot of practice. Right, we need to establish how far along you are with this pregnancy. As your periods have been so erratic lately, it's difficult to work out when the baby's due. Are you still feeling sick, dizzy, tired?'

'No. In fact, I've felt better than I have for a long time,' Diane declared.

'Hmm. It could be a sign that you're over twelve weeks or thereabouts. After that stage, a lot of women find that they no longer feel as sick or as tired, although everyone is different, of course.' She picked up her pen and made a note on Diane's file. 'I'll book you in for a scan, although the hospital usually prefers to do them at around sixteen weeks so they may decide to wait.'

'I'm happy to wait if it's better for the baby,' Diane said firmly and then frowned. 'There's a bigger risk of there being something wrong with it because of my age, isn't there?'

'Yes.' Beth knew that Diane would appreciate the truth rather than have her put a positive spin on the situation. 'The risk of having a child with Down's syndrome, for instance, increases with the mother's age. You will be offered tests to check for that.'

'I see.' Diane sounded momentarily worried before she rallied. 'Well, we'll have to wait and see what happens. There's no point borrowing trouble, is there?'

'Definitely not,' Beth agreed, thinking how well Diane was coping with the shock of it all. She could remember how she had felt when she had discovered she was pregnant, she thought as she saw Diane out. It had been a lot to take in, even though she had wanted a baby for so long. She sighed. Of course, it would have been different if Callum had still been there. They could have celebrated together, although *would* Callum have seen it as something to celebrate when he had no longer loved her? Now that Beatrix was a living, breathing human being, she didn't doubt that his feelings had changed about having a child but, back then, would he have seen her pregnancy as a hindrance that would stop him leaving her?

Beth felt a chill envelop her. Although she didn't doubt that Callum would have stayed with her if he'd known she'd fallen pregnant, it would have been out of a sense of duty and not out of love.

The computer problems slowed everything down so it was after seven before Callum left the surgery. He debated going round to see Beatrix but in the end decided not to risk it. He was still smarting at the thought of Beth going out with Owen Walsh and he needed to get a firm grip on his emotions before he spoke to her again.

He went up to the flat and made himself a meal of pasta and ready-made sauce then sat slumped in front of the television while he ate it. He felt tired and out of sorts and he knew that he had to shake himself out of this mood. Beth wasn't his any longer and he couldn't dictate what she did even if she would listen, which he very much doubted.

Part of her charm had always been her independence, her willingness to stand up for herself as well as for other people; why would he want her to change, even though he hated the thought of her seeing another man? He should be pleased that she was getting her life back on track but it was impossible to feel anything other than this bitter disappointment. It was a relief when the sound of his phone ringing cut through his unhappy thoughts and he snatched it up.

'Callum O'Neill.'

'It's me—Beth.'

'Beth,' he repeated as his thoughts spun even faster. He wouldn't change a single thing about her, apart from how she felt about him, of course. If he could make her love him again, as she had loved him once before, then he would do so in a trice. It was a revelation to realise how much he longed for it to happen so that it was a moment before he discovered that she was still speaking. 'Sorry, can you say that again?' he asked, forcing down the surge of pain at the sheer futility of hoping that she would ever feel that way about him again.

'Joe Thorne's just been on the phone. There's an elderly couple been reported missing. Apparently, they were planning to walk to the Witch's Cauldron and told the owner of the guest house where they're staying that they would be back by four but they've not appeared yet. Joe needs someone medically trained to go with the team. I can't go because of Beatrix and Daniel is at a meeting in Leeds so I suggested you.' She paused when he didn't reply. 'You don't have to go if you don't want to...'

'Of course I'll go.' Callum finally managed to drag his thoughts together, lining up the facts like ducks in a row: Joe Thorne, leader of the local search and rescue team; missing walkers, lost and possibly injured out on the hills; no one else available except him. 'Where are we meeting?' he demanded, dumping his plate on the coffee table.

'The car park at the lower edge of the Cascade, although Joe said he can pick you up on the way, if you want him to,' she informed him.

'Right,' Callum said, switching off the television. 'Can you phone Joe back and tell him I'm coming and that I'd like a lift? I don't have his number.'

'Of course.' She paused then rushed on. 'Take care, Callum.'

'I shall,' he replied, his heart swelling with joy because it seemed that she did care about him, after all. He opened his mouth to say something else, although heaven knew what, but realised that she had already hung up.

Hurrying into the bedroom, he gathered together what he would need, telling himself that it was ridiculous to get his hopes up like that. *Take care* was on a par with the equally anodyne *Have a nice day*—a trite comment that meant absolutely nothing. However, despite knowing that, he couldn't shake off the thought that Beth might actually *care* about him. A huge smile lit his face as he swung his backpack over his shoulder. Quite frankly, he couldn't think of a better inducement to get back safely!

Beth paced the sitting room floor, unable to settle. Although it was past midnight, she knew it was pointless trying to sleep. She kept thinking about Callum being out on the hills. Maybe he had worked in all sorts of places around the globe but the Yorkshire Dales were an unknown quantity to him. He had very little experience of the rough terrain he would encounter and she couldn't help worrying. He could so easily find himself in serious trouble.

The sound of a car drawing up outside had her flying to the window and she felt her heart leap with relief when she saw Callum getting out of the search and rescue team's four-wheel drive. Beth saw him glance towards the cottage and held her breath, wondering if he would knock on her door when he saw the light was on. It was only when she saw his shoulders slump as he turned away that she realised she couldn't let him leave without speaking to him. Hurrying to the front door, she called after him.

'Callum, wait! What happened? Did you find the missing walkers?'

'Yes, we did.' He came back and she could see the lines of strain etched on his face. Without pausing to think about what she was doing, Beth held the door wide open.

'Come in and tell me about it,' she said quietly. She led him into the sitting room and waved him towards a chair. 'I can see you're upset so what happened?'

He sighed heavily as he sat down. 'The woman was already dead when we found them. She had Alzheimer's disease, apparently, and had wandered off on her own and fallen over the edge of the Cauldron. Her husband had managed to climb down to her and he was just sitting there, holding her hand, when we arrived.'

'Oh, how tragic!' Beth declared, feeling her eyes sting with tears. 'It must have been horrendous.'

'It was. It took me ages to convince the husband that she was dead. He kept insisting that she'd be all right if we got her to the hospital.' He shook his head. 'Even after we'd loaded her body into the back of the car, he couldn't seem to take it in.'

'Where is he now?' Beth asked, her heart going out to him. A situation like this was always stressful and it was obvious that Callum had been deeply upset by what he had witnessed.

'Still at the hospital. He was in no fit state to be sent back to the B&B on his own,' he explained. 'The police have contacted his son and he's driving up here. He lives in Surrey, though, so it'll take him a while to get here.'

'At least the old man will have someone with him,' Beth said, softly. 'That will help.'

'Yes. He's lucky in that respect. At least he

isn't completely on his own now and has a family who cares about him.'

There was something in his voice that made Beth's heart ache all the more. Was Callum thinking that *he* didn't have any family who cared about him? She knew it was true and the urge to comfort him was too strong to resist. Reaching out, she gripped his hand. 'There are people who care about you, too, Callum.'

'Are there?' He gave a bitter laugh. 'If you mean my parents then forget it. They didn't care about me when I was a child and they certainly don't care about me now that I'm an adult.'

'You have friends,' she began but he shook his head.

'I've lost touch with most of my friends in the past year. I doubt they even spare me a thought these days. They have their own lives, their own problems—why should they worry about me?'

'Because they care about you! Maybe you haven't seen them for a while but it takes more than that to end a friendship.'

'Does it? Really? All it took to end our marriage were a few words, Beth. I told you I wanted a divorce and that was it.'

'That was different,' she murmured painfully. 'It was clear that you didn't want to be with me any more.'

'Was it? What if I only asked you for a divorce because I felt it was the right thing to do?'

'What do you mean?' She gripped his hand when he went to draw it away. 'Tell me, Callum!'

'Nothing. I'm just rambling, that's all.' He stood up, effectively breaking her hold on him. 'I'd better go. We've got work in the morning and it's late. I'm sorry if I woke you, Beth, but it was easier for Joe to drop me off here than drive to the surgery.'

'It doesn't matter,' she managed, her head reeling as she tried to make sense of what he had said.

What had Callum meant about it being the right thing to do? Right because he had stopped loving her? Or right for some other reason? She followed him into the hall, wishing that she could make him explain even though she knew it was pointless. The facts were clear, after all. Callum had stopped loving her and had asked her for a divorce.

And yet the nagging thought that she was missing something wouldn't go away. When he turned towards her, she searched his face, feeling her heart quicken when she saw the regret in his eyes, but regret about what? About divorcing her? But why would he regret it when it had been his decision?

'Callum,' she began.

'Don't.' He touched her mouth with his fingertips, stopping the question before it could emerge, and his expression was infinitely sad. 'There's really nothing more to say, Beth, believe me.'

He let himself out without another word. Beth watched until he disappeared from sight and only then did she let out the breath she hadn't realised she was holding. Closing the door, she leant back against it, feeling her whole body trembling. Raising her hand, she touched her mouth, but the warmth of Callum's fingers had already faded. She couldn't hold onto it any more than she had held onto him and it was the most bitter thought of all. She hadn't been enough for him and she never would be. Any interest he showed in her from now on was purely because she was the mother of his child. She took a deep breath, letting that thought seep into every cell in her body because she must never forget it.

Callum telephoned the hospital the following morning to check on the man he had helped to rescue and was relieved to hear that his son was now with him. He thanked the ward sister and hung up, wondering why the incident had had such an impact on him. Was it the fact that it had brought it home to him just how alone he was in the world? His only real family link was with Beatrix, his daughter, and he resolved to spend as much time as possible building a relationship with her.

When he went into work, he put through a call to Beth, meaning to start the way he needed to continue. Maybe the thought of her seeing another man devastated him, but if that was how things had to be, then he would use it to his advantage.

'Beth, it's me. I won't keep you because I'm sure you're busy, but I just wanted to say that if you need a babysitter any time then ask me. I'll be more than happy to mind Beatrix if you want to go out.'

'Oh. Right.' She sounded surprised, as well she might, Callum thought wryly. He had never imagined himself making such an offer.

'I know you said that you and Walsh might go out for dinner one night, so I thought I'd mention it,' he said, stamping on the spurt of jealousy that suddenly reared up inside him.

'I…er…yes, although we've not made any arrangements yet,' she said hurriedly.

'Well, when you do there's no need to worry about finding someone to look after Beatrix,' Callum said, hoping she couldn't hear the edge that had crept into his voice despite his best efforts to avoid it. 'I'll be happy to do it.'

'Um, thank you. Anyway, I'd better get on. Are you calling round tonight to see her?'

'If it's all right with you,' he said levelly.

'It's fine. I'll see you later then.'

With that she hung up, leaving Callum in a quandary. Whilst he was glad that he had made the offer, he couldn't claim that he was happy at the thought of her going out with Walsh, or anyone else for that matter. He sighed wearily. He couldn't have it both ways, could he? He couldn't offer to babysit and then behave like the proverbial dog in a manger. Beth was free to see whoever she liked, no matter how he felt about it. One thing was certain: Beth wasn't interested in having *him* back in her life in any capacity other than that of Beatrix's father. And even that wasn't guaranteed.

* * *

Beth was still reeling from the shock of Callum's phone call when she set out to visit one of the outlying farms that afternoon. It was a wet and windy day, the previously fine weather having changed in the space of a few hours as it often did in the Dales. Rain lashed against the windscreen as she headed out to Outhwaite's Farm.

Jenny Outhwaite had requested a home visit because she was worried about her youngest child, two-year-old Tilly, who was running a high temperature. It was the most remote of all the farms on their books and the journey there took time even on a good day. Now with the wind and rain slowing her down, Beth realised it was going to take her even longer than usual and sighed, wishing that she had phoned Alison to warn her that she might be late collecting Beatrix.

Maybe she should phone Callum and ask him to fetch her, she mused, and then just as quickly dismissed the idea. While she didn't doubt that he would take good care of Beatrix, was she really ready to make him an accepted part of her daughter's life? Apart from the concerns she had about his commitment, there was the fact that Callum unsettled her.

Take today, for instance. She'd felt on edge ever since he had offered his services as a babysitter. She wasn't sure why but it felt wrong to even think about asking him to look after Beatrix while she went out with another man. She sighed, knowing that she was overreacting. Hopefully, the situation would improve in time, but at the moment it seemed safer not to involve him in her affairs.

It turned out that little Tilly Outhwaite had chickenpox. The rash had appeared since Jenny had telephoned the surgery so Beth was quickly able to diagnose the problem. The little girl's chest and thighs were covered in spots, some of which had already turned into the fluid-filled blisters so characteristic of the illness. Beth advised Jenny to give Tilly paracetamol liquid for her temperature and to dab calamine cream on the spots to stop them itching. Cutting Tilly's nails would also help to prevent scarring if she scratched the scabs that would form once the spots started to heal.

Beth left the farm a short time later, having refused a cup of tea. The storm was getting worse and she was eager to get back to Beesdale. Rounding a bend in the road, she gasped when she was suddenly confronted by a huge pile of rocks blocking the way. She ground to a halt, her heart racing at the near miss she'd had.

Opening the car door, she went to investigate, hoping there would be room to drive around the landslide, but the ground beside the road was far too wet to risk it. Getting bogged down in the mud wouldn't help so her only option was to phone the surgery and see if Daniel could come out to collect her. Hurrying back to her car, she took her mobile phone out of its holder, groaning when she discovered that she didn't have a signal. There were blank spots all over the Dales and, typically, she was in the middle of one.

Beth got out of the car again and headed back along the road, holding up the phone in the hope that she could find a signal. Maybe it would help if she tried climbing up the hillside, she decided. She was in a dip here but if she was higher up then she might be able to connect to the nearest mast. Stepping off the road, she started to scramble up the hill. She was still staring at her phone and never even noticed the patch of loose rocks until her feet skidded out from under her. A searing pain shot through her right ankle as she fell heavily onto the ground and she cried out. Sitting up, she checked the damage, grimacing when she rolled up her trouser leg and discovered that her ankle was already swelling up. Whether it was sprained or broken, she couldn't tell, but the moment she tried to stand up and put her weight on it, the pain became unbearable.

Beth sank back down onto the ground, forcing back the tears as she suddenly realised her predicament. She couldn't get back to her car and return to the farm and she couldn't summon help either. It looked as though she was going to be stuck here until someone came looking for her.

If anyone did.

CHAPTER SEVEN

CALLUM WAS CLEARING up when Daniel came to find him. It had been a busy afternoon with appointments as well as the antenatal clinic. Polly had taken the clinic, but one of her mums had had a problem with her blood pressure and he had been drafted in to deal with it.

It had been a stark reminder of how easily things could go wrong during pregnancy. He knew from a comment Polly had passed that Beatrix had arrived several weeks early and it must have been a very worrying time for Beth. To say that he felt guilty about not being there was an understatement, even though he'd had no idea what had been happening at the time. He sighed because it all boiled down to one thing, didn't it? If he hadn't left in the first place, then he would have been here when Beth had needed him.

'Have you spoken to Beth recently?' Daniel asked him now without any preamble.

'Not since this morning, although I'm calling round to hers tonight to see Beatrix, as it happens.' Callum frowned when he saw the concern on the older man's face. 'Why? What's wrong?'

'I'm not sure,' Daniel replied. 'Alison has just phoned. Apparently, Beth hasn't collected Beatrix yet. Alison's quite happy to keep her there, but she's worried about Beth not turning up.'

'That's strange!' Callum exclaimed, glancing at his watch. 'It isn't like her to be late.'

'It isn't,' Daniel agreed. 'Apparently, she was doing a home visit this afternoon at Outhwaite's Farm. I've spoken to Jenny Outhwaite and, according to her, Beth left there a couple of hours ago.' He glanced out of the window and shook his head. 'The weather's atrocious so maybe that's what's delayed her.'

'I take it you've tried phoning her?' Callum said, his anxiety mounting. Maybe it was too soon to start panicking but it was hard not to do so.

'I have, but it's going straight to voice mail.' Daniel grimaced. 'The signal is patchy around there so it doesn't mean very much. She might just be out of range.'

'Or she could have had an accident.' Callum knew that he was merely voicing what Daniel was thinking and his heart turned over. He came to a swift decision, knowing that he wouldn't rest until he was sure that Beth was safe. 'I'll drive over there and see if I can spot her. Can you mark the route on the map for me? I've not been to the farm before and I don't want to end up getting lost.'

'Of course.' Daniel sounded relieved. 'I'll copy the map we have in Reception—all the farms are marked on there. Satnav's useless around here—you'll find yourself driving round in circles if you try to follow it. Stick to the map and you'll be fine.'

'Shall do.' Callum unhooked his waterproof jacket off the back of the door, thanking his lucky stars that he had left it there in case he ever needed it. The rain was lashing down now and the trees at the bottom of the car park were bent double from the force of the wind.

'Maybe I should come with you,' Daniel suggested suddenly. 'It's a filthy day and I don't want you going missing as well.'

'No, it's better if you stay here. That way you can alert the search and rescue team if you don't hear from me in a reasonable length of time.'

'Good point, although I hope that won't be necessary,' Daniel said grimly. 'I'll also phone Tim Outhwaite and ask him if he'll check if there's any sign of Beth thereabouts.'

'That would be a big help,' Callum agreed, heading for the door. They walked through to Reception where Daniel photocopied the section of the map that Callum needed, placing it in a plastic sleeve to keep it dry.

'Keep me posted, won't you?' he said, clapping Callum on the shoulder. 'I don't want anything happening to you.'

'Me neither,' Callum replied lightly, although there was no denying that Daniel's concern had sounded genuine. It reminded him of what Beth had said the other day about people caring about him. Maybe it was true, he conceded as he ran out to his car. However, the one person he really wanted to care about him was the most unlikely of all. After all, why should Beth care about him after the way he had behaved, even if he had believed that he was doing the right thing?

The thought stayed with him as he drove out of the town. The route was clearly marked and he had no difficulty following it, although he knew that he would have had problems if he hadn't had the map. The roads became increasingly narrow as he drove on, twisting and turning through the countryside. This part of the Dales was sparsely populated, with only the odd farm here and there, and he grew increasingly anxious when he saw no sign of Beth's car along the way. By his reckoning he was only a couple of miles away from Outhwaite's Farm now so where on earth was she?

He rounded a bend and had to slam on his brakes when he was confronted by a huge heap of rocks and soil blocking the road. It was obvious that the rain had caused a massive landslide and there was no way that he could drive around it. Leaving his car where it was, he hurried towards it, his feet slipping and sliding as he scrambled over the top, and felt his heart surge in relief when he saw Beth's car parked on the other side. He ran straight over to it, his relief rapidly disappearing when he discovered that it was empty. Fear knotted his guts as he turned in a slow circle and scoured the surrounding countryside. Where on earth was she?

Beth wasn't sure how long she had been stranded out on the hillside. The noise of the wind as it tore across the hills made it difficult to think clearly. All she knew was that the combination of the wind and driving rain had chilled her to the bone. The lightweight jacket she was wearing provided little protection from the elements and she knew that she needed to find shelter or she would be in real danger of developing hypothermia.

There was no way that she could walk so she tried scooting along on her bottom instead. It was sheer agony as even the slightest jolt sent a shaft of red-hot pain shooting through her ankle. In the end she couldn't do it any longer and was forced to stop. Pulling the collar of her jacket around her neck, she tried to conserve what little body heat she had left, but she was so cold now that her teeth were chattering. Glancing at her watch, she was shocked to see that it was gone seven o'clock. Hemsthwaite Surgery had closed after she had left to do the callout, and it was unlikely that anyone would have missed her. Although Alison was bound to wonder where she was when she didn't collect Beatrix; would she have raised the alarm?

And if so, would people know where to look for her? Tears welled in her eyes when it hit her that she might be stuck out there all night long.

'Beth!'

All of a sudden Callum was there beside her and Beth stared at him confusion. 'What are you doing here?'

'Looking for you, of course.' Stripping off his raincoat, he wrapped it around her. 'Explanations can wait for now. We need to get you out of this rain. Can you stand up?'

'No. I've injured my ankle.' She bit her lip, but it was impossible to hold back the sobs that rose up inside her.

'Shh, it's all right. You're safe now.' He drew her into his arms and Beth cried all the harder. Between the pain from her ankle and the fear that she might have been stranded on the hillside all night long, it was just too much.

'It's okay—you're safe now,' he repeated as he drew her closer. 'I know how scared you must have been, Beth, but it's all over now. We just need to get you to my car then I can drive you to the hospital and get your ankle seen to.'

'I didn't think anyone would miss me,' she muttered, brokenly.

'Of course we missed you,' Callum said hoarsely. He tilted her chin and Beth felt her heart leap when she saw the expression on his face, all the fear mingled with something else, an emotion that she had never expected to see. Callum was looking at her as though the thought of losing her was more than he could bear, but that couldn't be true. Could it?

When his head suddenly dipped, Beth closed her eyes. She didn't want to see anything else, didn't want to know if she was mistaken. She simply wanted him to kiss her and make her feel safe even though it defied all logic. Callum had left her. He had left her because he had no longer loved her. Those were the facts but she wasn't interested in facts at that moment, only in feelings: how Callum felt; how he made *her* feel. His lips found hers and she shud-

dered when she realised how cold they were—
the coldness of fear. When he parted her lips,
she didn't resist. She wanted to feel that chill
turn to warmth, feel fear turn to desire…

'Hello! Can you hear me? Where are you?'

The sound of a man's voice broke the spell.
Callum let her go and leapt to his feet as Tim
Outhwaite appeared. Beth took a shaky breath
but her heart was racing. She knew that in another second there would have been no turning
back. She would have given herself to Callum
right here on the hillside with the storm raging
around them. Had she learned nothing from
what had happened in the past? she thought,
bitterly. Apparently not!

'Thank heavens!' Tim came hurrying over to
them. 'I was starting to fear the worst when I
saw the cars and no sign of you both.'

'Beth's injured her ankle,' Callum informed
him tersely. 'I don't know if it's fractured or
sprained but we need to get her to hospital.'

Beth shivered when she heard the grating

note in his voice. Was Callum regretting what had happened just now? she wondered, sickly. Wishing that he hadn't behaved so impulsively? Maybe he had been tempted to kiss her but had it been the heat of the moment that had led him to behave that way? Callum hadn't wanted *her*. He had simply reacted to events.

Even though she knew it was foolish, she couldn't help feeling as though it was yet another rejection of her. It was only the thought of him guessing how devastated she felt that helped her hide her feelings as he and Tim carried her back to the road and got her settled in his car. Hurrying round to the boot, Callum took out an inflatable splint and carefully fitted it around her injured ankle.

'This should help protect it,' he said, steadfastly avoiding her eyes.

'Thank you,' Beth murmured, her heart aching all the harder when she realised she was right. Callum regretted what had happened because he was afraid of finding himself caught up in a situation he wouldn't welcome. It was a relief when he turned away to speak to Tim.

'Can you phone Dr Saunders and let him know that I'm taking Beth straight to the hospital? Her ankle will need X-raying and it's easier to go straight there.'

'Of course.' Tim grimaced. 'We've put you to an awful lot of trouble, Dr Andrews. I'm so sorry.'

'It isn't your fault,' Beth assured him, trying not to think about how hurt she felt. After all, nothing had changed. Callum may have reacted to the heat of the moment but it didn't alter the fact that he no longer loved her. She hurried on, determined not to go down that route. 'Can you ask Dr Saunders to phone Alison and explain what's happened and that I'll collect Beatrix as soon as I get back from the hospital?'

'I will.'

Beth sank back against the seat as they set off, feeling more exhausted than she'd felt in her entire life. Between the stress of being stuck out in the storm and what had happened with Callum, she felt completely drained. She glanced at him, studying the shape of his head and the set of his shoulders. Every detail was familiar to her. It had all been logged away in her brain, stored there for eternity. She had loved him so much but her love had meant nothing to him. Tears pricked her eyes. Even if they hadn't been interrupted, that kiss wouldn't have meant anything either.

What on earth had he been thinking?

Callum stood up and paced the corridor outside the X-ray department. Beth was inside having her ankle X-rayed. There was a red light above the door, warning people not to enter, and he sighed. If only there'd been a red light warning him of the danger of being so close to Beth again then he might not be in this situation now. However, the moment he had held Beth in arms, all sensible thoughts had fled. He had wanted to hold her and never stop. Wanted to kiss her and promise that she would never be in danger again as long as there was breath in his body. The urge to protect her had been over-whelming—so was that why he had behaved the way he had?

His heart lurched as he recalled what had hap-pened. It might have started out as an attempt to comfort her but there had been other emotions brewing, far stronger ones too. Holding Beth in his arms had unlocked all the feelings he had tried so desperately to forget. However, the thing that shocked him more than anything else was that he knew Beth wouldn't have stopped him kissing her. She hadn't tried to push him away, hadn't shown any sign at all that she hadn't wanted him to kiss her. She had simply looked at him and then closed her eyes…

The red light turned to green and Callum desperately tried to pull himself together as the radiographer wheeled Beth out. Allowing thoughts like that to fill his head was only ask-ing for trouble. Maybe she hadn't pushed him away but it didn't mean anything. After everything she had been through, she had needed comforting, and he'd just happened to be on hand.

'I have to see the doctor about my results,' she informed him tersely. 'I'm not sure how long it will take so don't feel that you have to wait for me. I can get a taxi home.'

'Of course I'll wait for you,' Callum said hotly, hurt beyond all reason that she should think that he would leave her to make her own way home. He pushed her back to A&E, his heart sinking when he realised once again what a poor opinion she must have of him. It made him see how foolish it would be to read anything into what had happened tonight. Beth had been scared and upset, and he'd been there. That was all.

It turned out that her ankle wasn't fractured but badly sprained. It would take a couple of weeks for it to heal and in the meantime Beth was not to put any weight on it. The doctor asked one of the nurses to strap it up then gave them a note for a pair of elbow crutches to be collected on their way out and that was that. Callum insisted on pushing her back to his car in the wheelchair then went back to fetch the crutches and stowed them in the back.

'Would you mind stopping off at Alison's so I can collect Beatrix?' Beth asked him as they set off.

'Of course not.'

Callum left the hospital, taking the ring road that skirted around the city centre. It would be quicker this way and he was eager to get home. Tonight had been tough and he needed time to get himself back on track. Telling Beth how he felt was out of the question: he could see that now. It was guaranteed to make her reconsider her decision to allow him to spend any time with Beatrix, so he needed to batten down his feelings no matter how difficult it was.

Thoughts flowed in and out of his head as he drove and he was thankful that Beth didn't seem to want to talk any more than he did. It was gone eleven when he drew up outside Alison's house. Beth immediately went to open the car door but he stopped her.

'You stay here—I'll fetch her. Remember what the doctor said about staying off your ankle.' He didn't wait for her to reply as he got out of the car and knocked on the door. Alison answered almost immediately, looking relieved when she saw him.

'Oh, good. You made it. I was wondering what to do if you didn't get back tonight. I don't have a cot now that the twins are that bit older, you see.'

'I'm sorry we're so late but it took quite a bit of time at the hospital,' Callum explained, following her inside. Beatrix was in the sitting room, listlessly playing with some toys. She smiled when she saw Callum and held up her arms to be picked up.

Callum swung her up into the air, feeling a whole rush of emotions hit him. He already loved her so much, this tiny miracle he had known nothing about until a few weeks ago. Losing her now would be unbearable and he would do anything to stop it happening. If he had to hide his feelings from Beth for ever then that was what he would do, because he simply couldn't risk losing his daughter for any reason.

It was a painful thought but one that needed to remain at the forefront of his mind, he realised as he carried Beatrix out to the car. Alison had offered to lend him a car seat as there wasn't one fitted in his car so he handed Beatrix to Beth while he secured it in the back. Once he was sure it was safely installed, he strapped Beatrix in and drove back to the cottage. Beth handed him the keys to the front door so he could carry a now sleeping Beatrix inside. He took her straight upstairs and placed her in her cot then went back to help Beth.

Using the crutches proved a bit of a problem so in the end he picked her up and carried her inside as well. He put her down next to the couch, quickly steadying her when she wobbled.

'Thanks,' she said, ruefully. 'I'll have to practise with these crutches. Obviously there's a knack to using them.'

'They probably need adjusting so they're the right height for you,' Callum said, trying to sound upbeat even though he couldn't help wondering how on earth she was going to manage. The stairs in the cottage, for instance, were extremely steep and he really couldn't see her being able to get up and down them even with the aid of the crutches.

Beth was obviously thinking the same as him because she sighed. 'I hope you're right, although I don't know how I'm going to make it up the stairs, let alone carry Beatrix up and down them. Maybe if I try doing it on my bottom, with her on my knee, it might work.'

'Would it be safe, though? I mean, if she starts squirming around then are you sure you can hold onto her?' Callum replied, anxiously.

'No. I'm not.' She frowned and he could see the worry on her face. 'I don't want to put her at risk in any way but what else can I do? I need to be able to bath and change her, put her in her cot—all the normal things I do each day.'

Callum took a deep breath. He had a bad feeling about what he was about to suggest but what choice did he have in the circumstances? 'Then it seems to me there's only one solution.'

'And that is?'

'That I move in here and help you.'

CHAPTER EIGHT

THE SKY OUTSIDE the sitting room window was grey and leaden, perfectly reflecting her mood. Beth lay on the couch thinking about what had happened and what she should do about it. Last night she had been too exhausted to argue when Callum had put his proposal to her but she knew that having him living in the cottage was the last thing she needed after what had happened yesterday. Maybe it had been a reaction to the stress of the situation, but there was no way that she was prepared to risk it happening again.

A light tap on the door made her jump and she pressed a hand to her throat to stem the sudden pounding of her pulse. 'Yes?'

'Can I come in?' Callum said quietly from

the other side of the door. 'Then I can make us some tea.'

'I…erm…yes,' Beth replied because it would be churlish to refuse. She pulled up the quilt, tucking it under her arms to hold it in place, then sighed. Did she really think that Callum would be so overcome with passion by the sight of her wearing her nightclothes that he wouldn't be able to control himself? Fat chance of that!

'How did you sleep, or did your ankle keep you awake?' he asked politely as he came into the room. It had been his idea that she should sleep on the couch. It converted into a double bed and was quite comfortable. The cottage had a downstairs loo plus a shower and it meant that she had everything to hand without needing to negotiate the stairs.

'It wasn't too bad,' Beth answered in the same vein. Maybe that was the key, she decided. Behave politely and steer clear of anything that could be construed as personal. It was worth a try so she carried on. 'I took another couple of painkillers around three a.m. and that seemed to settle things down.'

'Good.' He turned to go into the kitchen then paused. 'What time does Beatrix normally wake up? I popped my head round her door but she's still fast asleep so I left her.'

'She's usually wide awake by now!' Beth exclaimed. She tossed back the quilt as a rush of panic hit her. 'She is all right, isn't she? You did check that she was breathing properly?'

'There was no need,' he said quietly. 'It was obvious that she was asleep.'

'Obvious to you, maybe, but I need to check on her myself.' Beth swung her legs off the couch, completely forgetting about her ankle in her need to see her daughter. Pain shot through it when she tried to stand up and she gasped.

'For heaven's sake, Beth, be careful!' Callum caught her as she slumped forward and helped her sit down. 'If you keep putting pressure on that ankle, it will never heal.'

'I know but I need to see Beatrix and make

sure she's all right,' she said, raising haunted eyes to his face. 'You read about cot deaths and I have this awful fear that she might not wake up one day...' She broke off and Callum sighed.

'Oh, Beth, don't torture yourself. You know how rarely something like that happens.'

'Yes, but I can't help worrying. She means the world to me, Callum, and if anything happened to her, I just couldn't bear it.'

'That's how I feel too.' He bent so that he could look into her eyes. 'I've only known about her existence for a few weeks but I love her, too, Beth. She's the best thing that's ever happened to me.'

Beth knew what he was saying, that he was asking if she had made up her mind about allowing him to take on a more permanent role in their daughter's life. It was on the tip of her tongue to tell him that he could, but something held her back. Maybe he *did* love Beatrix, and maybe he *did* want to be her father, but would his interest last? She simply didn't know and it was the uncertainty that stopped her saying anything.

Disappointment crossed his face as he straightened up. 'I'll fetch her down then you can see for yourself that she's perfectly fine,' he said, his deep voice suddenly grating.

Beth watched him go with a heavy heart. She hated to know that she had upset him but she couldn't risk Beatrix's feelings. She had to be sure that Callum would stay the course before she allowed him to play a major role in their daughter's life. He came back a few moments later with Beatrix in his arms and placed her on the couch next to Beth.

'Here she is, a little grumpy 'cos she's been woken up, but otherwise she's fine. Give me a shout when you've finished having a cuddle and I'll take her into the kitchen for her breakfast. What does she normally have?'

'Porridge and a sliced banana,' Beth told him, hugging the baby close to her.

'Right. I'll go and get it ready.'

He turned to leave but Beth knew that she had to try to make amends for his disappointment.

'Thank you for doing this, Callum. You didn't have to stay and I appreciate it.'

'It's the least I can do.' He turned to look at her and there was a wealth of sadness in his eyes. 'I'll do anything it takes to prove to you that I can be a proper father to her, Beth, but, at the end of the day, it's your call. You have to decide if it's what you want too.'

He didn't wait to hear what she had to say, not that there was anything she could think of. Until she was one hundred per cent certain about his commitment then she couldn't make any promises and how could she ever be completely sure? Callum had sworn that he had loved her, hadn't he? That was why they had got married, because they had loved one another so much. Even though she had been devastated when he had told her that he'd wanted a divorce, a tiny bit of her had still believed that he'd cared about her. When he had come to see her after the divorce was finalised, and they had slept together, she had honestly thought that he had changed his mind and wanted her back. However, when she had woken up the following morning, he had gone.

Her heart ached as the memories came rushing back as bitter and as painful as ever. How could she believe a word he said after betraying her like that?

With Beth out of action, it put even more pressure on them at work. Callum agreed immediately when Daniel asked him if he would drive over to Hemsthwaite and work there until lunchtime. Anyone with an afternoon appointment would be offered the chance to be seen at The Larches instead. It wasn't ideal but it was the best they could do in the circumstances, although it was obvious that they couldn't continue running both surgeries with so few staff.

Callum left Daniel phoning around the agencies and drove over to Hemsthwaite. Hopefully,

Daniel would find someone to cover until Beth returned to work, although he didn't want her rushing back and end up hindering her recovery. He frowned. He didn't want her doing too much at home either. She had insisted on keeping Beatrix with her instead of taking her to Alison's, but he should have insisted that she stick to the arrangements. After all, childcare wasn't all down to Beth; he should take an active role in it too. He grimaced. Thinking like a parent didn't come easily to him.

Thankfully, he got through the morning without any major hiccups. One of his patients was a three-year-old boy who had chickenpox. It turned out that he went to the same playgroup as Tilly Outhwaite so no doubt he had caught it there and there would be other cases too. Although chickenpox was a fairly mild childhood illness and rarely caused complications, it could be extremely serious in the latter stages of pregnancy. Callum put through a call to the woman who ran the playgroup and explained what was happening so she could warn any expectant mums. There was no point putting people at risk.

He drove back to Beesdale after he had finished, pausing at the crossroads as he wondered if he should check on Beth. Although she had assured him that she would be fine, he didn't like to think of her being on her own with Beatrix all day. He drew up outside the cottage a few minutes later and let himself in, heading straight to the sitting room where he was met by a scene of chaos. There were toys everywhere—on the couch, on the coffee table, all over the floor. Beatrix was lying on the rug, fast asleep, while Beth was slumped on the couch. She looked up and he saw the tears in her eyes.

'I'm sorry it's such a mess. I've never known Beatrix to throw everything around like this before.'

'Hey, it's only some toys,' he said gently, going over to her. 'It won't take more than a few minutes to put them away.' He bent down, his heart aching when he saw how weary she looked. 'How are you doing? That's the main thing. Is your ankle all right?'

'Yes,' she began then grimaced. 'Not really. I didn't like to take the painkillers in case they made me feel a bit woozy and my ankle is throbbing like crazy now.'

'You need to take them every four hours,' Callum said firmly. 'If you let the pain get too bad then it will just take longer for it to die down.'

'I know.' She sighed. 'I was just worried in case I wasn't in a fit state to look after Beatrix.'

'I can understand that but you still need to take them.' Callum lifted them down from the shelf and handed them to her. 'I'll fetch you some water.'

He went into the kitchen and filled a glass with water, wishing that he had thought about this before. Beth was bound to be wary of taking the tablets if she thought they could affect her ability to look after their daughter. A fine doctor he was not to think about that, he thought wryly, not that he wanted to be Beth's doctor, of course.

The thought of exactly what he would like to be was something he knew that he mustn't dwell on. The situation was volatile enough as it was. Although Beth had spent the night on the sofa, he had been very conscious of the fact that he'd been sleeping in the bed they had once shared. He wouldn't have been human if he hadn't re-called how different life had been before the strain of trying for a baby had affected them.

Making love with Beth had been everything he could have dreamed about, their passion for one another reaching heights that he had never known existed before. He had loved her with both his heart and his soul and the thought filled him with a deep sense of regret for all he had lost. It was an effort not to show how he felt as he took the glass of water through to the sit-ting room. However, the last thing he needed was Beth noticing he was upset, and wonder-ing about it.

'Here you are.'

'Thanks.' Beth downed the tablets then leant back against the cushions with another sigh. 'I can't wait for them to kick in.'

'I bet you can't,' he said, sympathetically. 'Right, now that's sorted, how about I make you something to eat? What do you fancy?'

'Anything. I'm famished, but are you sure you've got time?' she said, glancing at her watch.

'Yes, well, enough time to make you a sandwich. The cordon bleu meal will have to wait until another day, I'm afraid,' he replied, drolly.

Beth laughed out loud. 'Since when did you start cooking cordon bleu meals? Eggs and bacon were your speciality. It's the only thing you ever made for us.'

Beth knew she'd made a mistake the moment the words were out of her mouth but there was nothing she could do about it. She couldn't *un*say them, couldn't pretend that she remembered nothing about the time when they had lived together.

'Hmm, cooking's definitely not one of my major accomplishments,' he agreed, ruefully. 'It's a good job you could cook, Beth, or we'd have starved.'

'I doubt it,' she said quickly, not wanting to go down the slippery slope of remembering all the cosy evenings they had spent, enjoying meals she had made for them. It would only lead to the next memory about how those evenings had ended, with them in bed together. Pain seared through her and she hurried on. 'I'm sure you would have managed to make something, even if it was only beans on toast.'

'Maybe. Anyway, I'd better go and rustle something up for you,' he said flatly, and she had a feeling that he was as keen as she was to change the subject. 'Should I make something for Beatrix as well?'

'No, she's already had her lunch,' Beth explained, quietly. Had Callum been thinking the same as her? she wondered as he disappeared into the kitchen. Remembering how wonderful their life had been? She knew it was true and it hurt to know how much things had changed. She had honestly thought that they would be together for ever but she'd been wrong. Their love hadn't been strong enough to withstand the pressures of them trying to conceive. How ironic that what had led to the break-up of their marriage had brought them back together. If she hadn't given birth to their daughter then Callum would never have contacted her again.

It was hard to shake off the feeling of melancholy that thought aroused when he came back with a plate of sandwiches and a mug of coffee but Beth knew that she had to keep things on an even footing. She frowned when he set the plate and mug on the table beside her. 'Aren't you having anything?'

'I've not got time. I covered Hemsthwaite Surgery this morning but I'm needed at The Larches this afternoon so we've had to close

Hemsthwaite early.' He shrugged. 'We simply don't have enough staff to run both surgeries.'

'It's a nightmare, isn't it?' Beth said, worriedly. 'Is Daniel trying to find locum cover?'

'He was phoning around the agencies this morning when I left,' Callum explained.

'How on earth will you manage if he doesn't find anyone? I suppose I could come in. I mean, if I just sit at my desk then it won't affect my ankle, will it?'

He shook his head. 'You know it isn't as simple as that, Beth. You'll have to get up to fetch things and examine patients. All it needs is for you to go over on that ankle and you could be out of action for months. No, you need to be sensible and rest it, which is why I was going to suggest that I drop Beatrix off at Alison's on my way to the surgery. It would be easier if she was there, wouldn't it?'

'I suppose so,' Beth conceded. 'I thought I could cope but after this morning, I'm not so sure. She's run me ragged!'

Callum laughed. 'Don't sound so disgusted. You aren't the only mum who needs a helping hand, especially at a time like this.'

'Maybe not but I just feel that I should be able to cope.'

'You can and you do cope wonderfully. But sometimes you have to accept that you can't do it all yourself and this is one of those times.' He paused then carried on. 'It isn't just down to you, Beth, or it shouldn't be. Beatrix is my responsibility too.'

'But for how long, though? Until my ankle's better? Or until you grow tired of being responsible for her?'

'You still don't believe that my interest will last, do you?' he said harshly.

'No, I don't, if you want the truth.' She spread her hands wide open. 'Oh, you seem keen enough right now but who knows how you'll feel in six months' time?'

'I don't know how to convince you that I mean what I say,' he began, but she cut him off.

'Oh, I'm sure you mean it at this very moment, but you could change your mind. After all, it wouldn't be the first time, would it?'

'Meaning when I asked you for a divorce? You're never going to believe that I had my reasons for doing what I did, are you, Beth?'

The bitterness in his voice surprised her and she frowned. After all, it had been Callum's decision to end their marriage, so why should he sound so upset about it? It was on the tip of her tongue to ask him but she managed to hold back. Did she really want to go down that route again, start looking for excuses for his behaviour? She had done that in the months after he had left, dreamt up increasingly bizarre explanations as to why he had gone, and she refused to do it again. Callum had left because he had stopped loving her, and that was all she needed to know.

'Quite frankly, I don't care what your reasons were, Callum. The only thing that concerns me now is making sure you don't do the same thing to Beatrix.'

'I won't.'

'No, you won't because I won't let you.'

'So that's it then, is it? You're not even going to give me a chance to prove that I mean what I say?' he said, hotly.

'Do you blame me?' she countered, just as hotly. 'Why would I want to take the risk of Beatrix getting hurt?'

'Because I will never, *ever* hurt her! She's my daughter and I'll do whatever it takes to make sure she's safe and happy.'

'Even if it means staying in Beesdale for the rest of your life?' she said, sceptically.

'Yes! If that's what it takes then that's what I'll do.' He bent so that he could look into her eyes and Beth shivered when she saw the anguish on his face. 'This is more important than anything else and I only wish I could convince you of that.'

'And I wish I could believe you, but I can't.'

Beth could feel her own emotions bubbling up inside her, all the pain and heartache she had felt after Callum had left her coming together to form a huge torrent that threatened to overwhelm her.

'Then it seems we've reached an impasse.' He straightened abruptly. 'I just hope you don't regret your decision when Beatrix is old enough to start asking why she doesn't see her father. Admitting that you stopped me having any contact with her might not go down too well with her.'

'If that's a threat——' she began.

'It isn't. It's merely a statement of fact. Maybe you need to think about it.'

He didn't say anything else as he picked up Beatrix and carried her out to his car. Beth watched them go with a heavy heart. She didn't want to be at odds with him but it was obvious that they saw the situation from two very different perspectives. She sighed as she started to clear away the toys. Callum seemed so sure that he would stay the course but would he? He had spent most of his life since he had qualified working overseas and she simply couldn't imagine him settling down to life as a rural GP. He might be content enough for a while but at some point the need to move on was bound to surface and she could imagine how devastated Beatrix would be if he disappeared from her life when she had grown to love him. Even if it was difficult to answer Beatrix's questions in the future, it was a risk she wasn't prepared to take for any reason. Or anyone.

The days flew past and the spell of bad weather gradually improved. Callum woke to blue skies on the Saturday morning but it did little to improve his mood. Relations between him and Beth had hit an all-time low and they were barely speaking now. Fortunately, her ankle was healing and she was much more mobile now, although she still had difficulty negotiating the stairs. He knew that once she was able to manage them, she would insist she didn't need his help, so his time at the cottage was limited.

Although he loved the fact that he got to spend so much time with his daughter, he couldn't deny that he found it stressful. Being in the cottage had brought back a lot of memories, both good and bad, and he wouldn't have been human if he hadn't found himself thinking about what had gone on there and regretting it.

Beatrix didn't go to Alison's at the weekend. Callum knew that Beth would claim that she could manage on her own and didn't need his help, but he had no intention of leaving her to fend for herself all day long. It was just gone seven when he went into the nursery, smiling when he discovered that Beatrix was wide awake.

'Good morning, madam, and how are you this fine day? Full of beans from the look of you.'

Lifting her out of the cot, he dropped a kiss on the top of her head, feeling his insides scrunch up with love. Although he had treated many children in the course of his work, he'd had very little to do with them on a personal level, and he hadn't expected to feel this way. It made him see how important it was that he and Beth resolve their issues. He needed to be part of his daughter's life, not just for her sake but for his as well, and to do that he had to convince Beth that she could trust him, although how he was going to achieve that was a mystery. He was still mulling it over when he carried Beatrix into the kitchen and popped her in her high chair.

'Oh, I didn't know you were in here.'

Callum swung round when he heard Beth's voice. Just for a second his senses whirled as he took stock of what she was wearing, which was very little. In a fast sweep his eyes ran over her, drinking in the sight she made as she stood there dressed only in a pale blue bath towel. It was only when he realised that she was waiting for him to say something that he managed to drag his thoughts together, but it was an effort.

The sight of her near-naked body was definitely having an effect on him!

'I...er... I thought you were in the shower,' he murmured, desperately trying to clamp down on the surge of desire that was racing through him.

'I just got out,' she said, then suddenly seemed to realise her state of undress. Colour bloomed in her cheeks as she swung round and hobbled out of the kitchen. 'I'd better get dressed.'

Not on my account, Callum wanted to say, but managed to stop himself. He needed to heal this rift between them, not make it bigger. 'And I'd better give this little lady her breakfast.'

He got everything ready, forcing himself to concentrate on what he was doing and nothing else. Thinking about how beautiful Beth had looked in that scanty little towel certainly wouldn't damp down his raging hormones. By the time Beth reappeared, Beatrix had finished her porridge and was eating a banana, squeezing the fruit so that it oozed between her fingers.

'I think she prefers mashed banana,' he said, desperately trying to keep his thoughts on his daughter's antics. Maybe he did want Beth but it wouldn't help his case one iota if he let her know that.

'So I can see.' Beth tore off a length of kitchen roll and wiped the baby's hands. 'You're supposed to eat it, darling, not squeeze it to death. You're such a mucky little thing!'

Callum laughed as he took the empty cereal bowl over to the sink. 'She'll grow out of it eventually, I expect.'

'I hope so.'

Beth rolled her eyes as she sank down onto a chair and Callum felt his heart lift just a little. She didn't appear quite so hostile this morning and he had to admit that it was a relief not to be treated like a pariah for once. Maybe they could arrive at a compromise, he thought as he washed the bowl and put it back in the cupboard. If they tried talking to one another rather than arguing all the time, then surely she would start to trust him? It was that thought that made him make a suggestion he had never planned on making.

'How would you feel about having a day out?' He turned to face her, feeling his emotions swirl once more. It had nothing to do with how she was dressed this time but how she had always affected him. Right from the beginning he'd only had to look at her to want her and it was disconcerting to realise how little his feelings had changed.

'A day out,' she repeated. 'You mean go some-where, together?'

'Yes.' He shrugged, trying to keep a tight grip on his emotions. 'Your ankle's a lot better and so long as you don't do too much then it should be fine. I'm sure Beatrix would enjoy a change of scene so why don't we take her out for the day?'

'I'm not sure if it's a good idea,' she began.

'It's just a day out, Beth. I'm not suggesting that we bury the hatchet, although I'm more

than willing to do so if that's what you want.'
He sighed when she didn't say anything. 'I just
feel it might make things…well, easier if we at
least tried to get along. So what do you say?'

CHAPTER NINE

THEY WENT TO a petting zoo the other side of Hemsthwaite. Callum had found it online and suggested that it would be the perfect place for Beatrix. She certainly seemed to be enjoying herself, Beth thought, listening to her daughter squeal with excitement when she saw the goats. Callum lifted her out of the pushchair and held her close to the fence so that she could stroke their whiskery faces, and Beth frowned. For someone who knew very little about children, Callum seemed to have struck just the right note by bringing them here.

It was an unsettling thought, especially when it made her realise how hard she had been on him lately. Maybe she did have concerns about his ability to commit to being a father, but there was no doubt that he was making a huge effort to live up to the role. She summoned a smile when he brought Beatrix over to where she was sitting, feeling guilty all of a sudden. She hated to think that she was being unfair to him.

'She's certainly enjoying herself. I've never heard her squeal like that before.'

'The goats are obviously a big hit,' Callum agreed, laughing when Beatrix started wriggling around, demanding to be put down. 'Oh, off we go again. Are you all right sitting there for now? There's llamas over there but the ground looks rather rough and I don't want you coming a cropper.'

'I'm fine,' Beth assured him, trying not to read anything into the way he was treating her with such concern, but it was impossible not to do so. A rush of warmth invaded her and it took all her effort not to let him see how touched she felt. 'I'll sit here till you come back then maybe we can go to the café. It's almost time for Beatrix's lunch so we may as well have something to eat as well.'

'Good idea.' He set Beatrix on the ground and took firm hold of her hand. 'Come on then, sunshine, let's see what you make of those llamas. You won't see many of them roaming around the Dales!'

Beth watched him lead Beatrix towards the llamas' pen. There were a lot of families there enjoying a day out and she couldn't help thinking how well Callum fitted in. Nobody watching him and Beatrix would guess that he had only known about his daughter for such a short time. She sighed because it would be a mistake to allow appearances to influence her. Although he seemed to be adapting to the role of doting father, she still wasn't convinced his interest would last. And nobody, not even Callum himself, could guarantee that it would.

The café was crowded but Callum managed to find them a table outside on the terrace. He got

Beth seated then fetched a highchair for Beatrix and popped her in it. 'Right, what do you fancy?'

'Just coffee and a sandwich is fine for me, thank you. I've brought Beatrix's lunch with me. There's a jar in the bag and it just needs warming up.'

'I'll do that first then,' he said, taking the jar of baby food out of the bag. There was a flask of juice in there as well and he handed it to Beth to open, smiling when Beatrix immediately reached for it. 'I expect she's thirsty after all the excitement.'

'I expect she is.' Beth loosened the top on the flask and handed it to her daughter. She laughed when Beatrix began to gulp it down. 'Hmm, you're right. All that squealing has obviously built up a thirst.'

'I could do with a coffee myself,' Callum admitted and rolled his eyes. 'I didn't realise it was such thirsty work, having fun.'

He grinned at her and Beth felt her heart give

a little bounce when she realised how handsome he looked when he smiled like that. Ever since Callum had come back to Beesdale they had been at loggerheads, it seemed, and there had been very little to smile about. Now she could feel her pulse racing and it was unnerving to know that he still had this effect on her. It was a relief when he went to heat up the baby food because it gave her a breathing space. Maybe she was still attracted to him but nothing would come of it. She wasn't foolish enough to risk having him break her heart a second time.

Callum could feel his heart pounding as he paid for their lunch. He couldn't rid himself of the memory of how Beth had looked at him. Had he made a mistake or had there been genuine awareness in her eyes just now? A shudder ran through him as he took his change from the cashier. He knew how dangerous it was to think like that. It would only lead to other thoughts, ones he couldn't afford to harbour. It wasn't how he felt about Beth that mattered; it wasn't even how she felt about him. It was whether she would allow him to be Beatrix's father that was the issue. He simply couldn't risk alienating her by doing or saying the wrong thing.

His heart was heavy as he carried the tray outside to their table. It wasn't going to be easy to hide his feelings but he knew it was what he needed to do. He had hurt her badly when he had left, even though he had truly believed it had been the right thing to do. However, even if he explained it all to her, would she believe him? It was obvious that she didn't trust him and she could think that he was simply spinning her a tale. Although he longed to tell her the truth, he was afraid that he might end up making the situation worse. He sighed. It would be better not to say anything than run that risk.

'Here we go. I'm afraid there wasn't much choice, so it's tuna mayo or cheese and pickle— take your pick,' he said with forced cheerfulness as he placed the tray on the table.

'I'll have the cheese if you don't mind,' Beth

replied, taking one of the cardboard cartons of sandwiches.

'No problem.' Callum doled out coffee and paper napkins then sat down. Beatrix had finished her lunch and was eating some strawberries now. Picking up a napkin, he wiped away a dribble of juice that was trickling down her chin. 'There you go, poppet. All beautiful again.' He dropped a kiss on the end of her nose and picked up his coffee, only then realising that Beth was watching him with the strangest expression on her face. 'What's the matter?' he said, wondering what he had done wrong this time.

'Nothing.' She bit her lip but he could tell that she was holding something back and it made him more determined than ever to make her tell him.

'Oh, come on! It's obvious that you want to say something, so out with it. It's not like you to pull your punches, Beth. Or not lately, at least.'

She flushed bright red. 'If I haven't pulled my

punches then it's because I wanted to make the situation perfectly clear to you, Callum. You came back here expecting to step into the role of Beatrix's father, but it isn't as simple as that.'

'So I've gathered,' he replied, tartly.

'Good.' She tilted her head and looked him straight in the eyes. 'At least we've made some progress.'

'You may have done but I certainly haven't. And I won't until you accept that I'm serious about this.' He held up his hand when she went to interrupt. 'No, I've heard it all before, Beth. You've made it perfectly plain that you don't believe I'll last the course. But you can't prove that I'm going to jump ship any more than I can prove that I won't.' He laughed harshly, unable to hide his frustration.

'I knew it wasn't going to be easy when I came back here but I never thought you'd have such a closed mind. You're so determined to punish me for leaving you that you don't care about the impact it's going to have on our daughter if you won't allow me to be a father to her!'

The accusation cut her to the quick. Beth reeled back, appalled that Callum could even think that. Beatrix was her first and only concern...wasn't she? The doubt rushed in before she could stop it, growing stronger by the second. Was she thinking solely about her daughter or was she also thinking about herself, about how devastated she'd been when Callum had left her? She couldn't put her hand on her heart and swear it wasn't true and she felt sickness well up inside her at the thought that she might be guilty of basing her decision on her own feelings rather than on Beatrix's needs.

'I'm sorry. I shouldn't have said that.'

Beth looked up, unable to hide how upset she felt. 'Why not if it's what you believe?' she replied, brokenly.

'It isn't. Well, I suppose I do think it's partly true. What happened between us is a huge sticking point, although I suppose it's only to be expected.' He sighed as he reached over the table and caught hold of her hand. 'I know you feel that I let you down, Beth, but I did it for the very best of reasons.'

'What reasons? You keep hinting that there was more to your decision to ask me for a divorce than the fact that you'd fallen out of love with me, so tell me what it was. You owe me that much, at least, Callum.'

She snatched her hand away, not wanting him to touch her. Her heart was pounding as she waited to hear what he had to say, even though she couldn't imagine what it would be. It was all quite simple to her mind: if Callum had loved her, he would never have divorced her and left. So how on earth was he going to explain what he had done?

'It wasn't an easy decision,' he began then stopped when another family came and sat down at the table next to theirs. There were four young boys in the group and they immediately started squabbling over a plate of giant cookies. The youngest boy grabbed one of the cookies and bit into it then suddenly toppled off his chair, clutching his throat. The two adults appeared rooted to the spot with shock, so Callum leapt to his feet. Kneeling down beside the child, he rolled him over and checked his airway, although he could see the piece of cookie lying on the floor next to him. It was obvious that the boy hadn't swallowed it but there was no doubt that he was having difficulty breathing.

Callum turned to the couple. 'I'm a doctor. Is he allergic to anything? He didn't eat any of the cookie—the piece he bit off is here on the floor. I think he must be allergic to something it contains.'

'Nuts.' The woman suddenly seemed to rouse herself. She shot to her feet. 'He's my nephew, you see, and my sister keeps going on about him being allergic to nuts. I just thought she was fussing...' She broke off and Callum sighed. However, now wasn't the time to point out how foolish it had been to ignore the warning. The boy's breathing was becoming even more laboured as his airway went into spasm.

'Did your sister give you anything in case this ever happened?' he demanded. 'Something that looks like a pen and contains a drug you can inject him with.'

'Yes, yes, she did! It's in my bag.' She grabbed hold of her bag and emptied it onto the table. 'Help me find it, Don,' she shouted to her husband, scrabbling through the heap.

'There it is.' Reaching over, Callum grasped the preloaded injection of adrenaline and plunged it into the child's thigh, praying that it would work. His heart sank when he realised that the boy's breathing wasn't improving. He was obviously going to need a second shot and there was always the danger that he could arrest in the meantime.

Glancing around, he spotted the girl who worked on the till and called her over. 'I'm a doctor and I need you to fetch my bag out of my car.' He told her the registration number and where it was parked then handed her the keys. 'Before you go, do you know if there's a defibrillator on site? He's a very sick little boy and we may need it.'

'I think there is, but I don't know where it's kept,' the girl explained. 'I'll get one of the others to ask the manager.'

She hurried away as Callum turned back to the child. He looked up when Beth came to join him.

'I've phoned for an ambulance.'

'Let's hope it gets here in time,' he said, quietly, as she knelt down beside him. 'I don't like the look of him at all.'

The words were barely out of his mouth when the child's eyes suddenly rolled back and he stopped breathing. Callum bent over him, shaking his head as he checked for a pulse. 'Nothing. We'll have to start CPR. Apparently, there's a defibrillator somewhere in this place but only the manager knows where it is.'

'Not much use hiding it away,' Beth said, tartly. 'I'll do the breathing if you'll do the compressions.'

She placed her mouth over the child's mouth and gave two sharp inflations. Callum followed them up with the necessary chest compressions. A crowd had started to gather now and they fell silent when they realised what was happening. They carried on like that for several minutes before the manager appeared carrying the portable defibrillator.

'I keep it locked up in the office,' the man explained importantly, placing it next to them. 'It'd be such a shame if people started messing around with it.'

'It'd be an even bigger shame if someone died because nobody knew where to find it,' Callum stated, bluntly.

He and Beth carried on performing CPR while the manager set up the defibrillator. The young cashier had come back with his bag and, without him even needing to ask, Beth took over the compressions while he drew up a second shot of adrenaline. Callum plunged the needle into the child's thigh then picked up the defibrillator paddles and applied them to the boy's chest, sending up a silent prayer. With the ambulance taking so long to reach them, he didn't rate the child's chances if this didn't work. When the boy suddenly coughed, Callum felt his heart lift in relief.

'It's all right,' he said soothingly when the boy started to cry. 'You're going to be fine now. Just try to breathe nice and steadily for me.'

He checked the boy's pulse again and was reassured to find that it was growing stronger by the second. He moved aside when the boy's aunt came and knelt down beside them. Beth looked exhausted as she struggled to her feet and he helped her back to their table where Beatrix was still sitting happily in the highchair, playing with a toy.

'I don't want to go through anything like that

again in a hurry,' she declared, running a trembling hand over her face.

'Me neither,' he agreed. Performing CPR was both physically and emotionally draining and it didn't get any easier no matter how many times you were called upon to do it.

'I really thought we were going to lose him at one point,' she said, her voice catching.

'So did I.' Callum put his arm around her, feeling more than a little choked up himself. Now that he had a child of his own, he understood just how awful it must be to lose a precious son or daughter. 'But we didn't, Beth, and it's mainly thanks to you. You did a great job just now. It isn't easy doing both the breathing and the compressions.'

She shook her head. 'No, it was a team effort.'

'We always did make a great team,' Callum said without thinking. It was only when she lifted anguished eyes to his that he realised what he had said, but it was too late to take it back by then. Far too late to pretend that he hadn't meant it either.

'Then why did you leave me, Callum? If we were such a great team, what made you change your mind about us? I think I deserve to know the answer, don't you?'

The ambulance arrived some thirty minutes later, by which time the little boy, Harley Mitchel, was breathing steadily and seemed none the worse for his adventures. It was obvious that his aunt and uncle were loath to spend the rest of the day at the hospital, but Callum insisted that Harley needed to be checked over. Beth had never heard him take such a tough stance before and it was a surprise, yet why should it be? Callum could be ruthless when the need arose, as she knew to her cost.

The thought sent a shiver of apprehension racing through her as they gathered up their belongings and left. Although she'd been the one to demand an explanation from him, she was no longer sure if she wanted to hear what Callum had to say. After all, what would it achieve at this point? There was no guarantee that it would make the situation any easier, although it could make it a lot worse.

For one thing, she had never even considered the idea that Callum had left her for another woman. They had both lived and worked together, so how would he have found the time for an affair? However, they had started leading separate lives after he had asked her for a divorce and she suddenly wondered if he could have met someone then. Her heart scrunched up inside her because she could imagine how devastated she was going to feel if he told that he had fallen *out* of love with her and *in* love with someone else. By the time they arrived back at the cottage, she was beginning to wish that she had never started this conversation.

'Shall I take Beatrix straight upstairs and bath her?' Callum asked as he carried the little girl inside. He grimaced. 'She's completely worn out after all the excitement today.'

'Please. She can have an early night,' Beth said, struggling to stay calm. Although the idea of Callum loving another woman was terrifying, she would have to deal with it if it turned out to be true. However, there was no denying that it could have a huge bearing on what happened in the future. If he was in love with someone else, and thinking about marrying her, then she needed to know.

It was hard not to panic at the thought of some other woman being added to the equation. She tried to push the thought to the back of her mind as she went into the kitchen to make Beatrix's tea but it was impossible. Even if Callum wasn't involved with anyone at the moment, it could happen in the future.

How did she feel about Beatrix having another family, a stepmother and possibly even half-siblings? What if Beatrix found herself pushed to one side? One heard about such things and it could very well happen. By the time Callum came back downstairs with Beatrix, Beth had worked herself up into a real state. No way was her daughter going to be made to feel that she was second best.

Callum made a pot of coffee while Beth helped Beatrix eat her tea. By tacit consent, neither of them mentioned the subject uppermost in their minds. Beatrix's eyelids were drooping by the time she had finished the last fish finger and Beth sighed.

'I think we'll skip dessert tonight. She's too tired to bother eating it from the look of her.'

'I'll take her up and put her in her cot,' Callum said gruffly.

Beth shivered when she heard the strain in his voice. Was he thinking about their forthcoming conversation? she wondered, sickly. Feeling nervous about what he had to tell her? She knew it was true and it simply intensified her fears. Maybe it was foolish, but it was going to hurt unbearably if he had found someone else.

'I think you'd better.'

Beth dropped a kiss on her daughter's head, feeling all the love welling up inside her. Finding out that she was pregnant after Callum had left had been a huge shock. After everything they had been through to have a baby, it had seemed incredible that it should have happened like that. However, even if Callum had met somebody else, she didn't regret having Beatrix. She was her own little miracle, the child Beth had given up any hope of having.

No matter how painful this situation turned out to be, she was incredibly lucky to have her and she would keep that in mind. When Callum came back downstairs, she turned to face him because there was no point putting it off any longer.

'So, why did you really leave me, Callum? I think it's time you told me the truth.'

Callum picked up the coffee pot even though the last thing he wanted was anything to drink. It was merely a delaying tactic to give him time to work out what he should say. He sighed when it struck him that they had gone way beyond that point now. It was obvious that Beth was determined to get to the bottom of this mystery and no amount of carefully chosen words were going to help.

'Because I thought it was the best thing to do,' he said flatly, putting the pot back on the table. 'Things had become so fraught that I was afraid you could no longer cope.'

'Fraught,' Beth echoed, staring at him. 'I don't understand.'

'Of course you do!' he said hotly, then took a deep breath, knowing that he had to explain his reasons calmly and rationally. Getting upset certainly wouldn't help to convince her that he had done the right thing—the *only* thing possible in the circumstances.

His tone was gentler when he continued, his emotions held strictly in check. 'Getting pregnant had become, well, an obsession for you—you couldn't think about anything else. I was afraid that you wouldn't be able to handle it if it turned out that we could never have a child and that's why I left. With me off the scene, you'd have to stop and think about what you were doing.

'However, if I stayed, we'd be forever trapped on the merry-go-round, forever trying to have the child you longed for. I did it for you, Beth. I did it because I loved you and couldn't bear to watch you ruining your life any more.'

'And you really expect me to believe that?' She laughed harshly, twin spots of colour burning in her cheeks. 'You left because you loved me and you wanted to save my sanity?'

'I didn't say that,' he began, his heart sinking because this wasn't going at all well.

'Not in so many words, but it's what you meant, Callum. I was *obsessed* with having a child and you thought I wouldn't be able to *cope* if it didn't happen. No wonder you wanted out. I mean, it wasn't as though you were ever that keen for us to have a baby. Oh, you went along with it but it was more to please me than out of any real desire on your part.' She smiled thinly. 'I can understand why you chose to leave when the going got tough.'

'That's not true!' How on earth was he going to convince her that she was wrong? he wondered desperately. He had left for *her* sake and not because he had grown tired of the situation.

'Oh, but I think it is true. You'd had enough and you wanted out. The fact that I got pregnant that last night we slept together is incidental. It certainly doesn't mean that you've changed. You would do the same thing all over again if it suited you.'

'You're wrong, completely wrong. I left for your sake, Beth, not mine, and that's the truth.' He took a deep breath, trying to clamp down on his emotions so that he could convince her. 'If I'd had any idea that you would find yourself pregnant after we slept together that night then I would never have left.'

'I'm sure you wouldn't. You'd have done your

duty, wouldn't you, Callum, and stayed? Or at least stayed until the joys of fatherhood started to pall.'

'That would never have happened,' he declared. 'I would never have left you to bring up our child on your own.'

'No?' She shrugged. 'I suppose we'll never know now, will we? I can't prove that you would have left and you can't prove that you would have stayed. However, it does make me see what a risk it would be to ever rely on you again.'

'What do you mean?' he asked, his stomach churning because he had already guessed what she was about to say.

'That allowing you to be part of Beatrix's life is far too dangerous. To be blunt, I don't trust you, Callum, and nothing you've told me tonight has made me change my mind.'

Her voice caught on a sob as emotion suddenly got the better of her and Callum felt a huge great wave of guilt wash over him. He couldn't bear to witness her anguish and know that he was responsible for it. He got up, crouching down in front of her chair. Beth was hurting and all he wanted at that moment was to comfort her.

'Every word I said was true, Beth. I left because I honestly thought it was the best thing to do.' He captured her hands, overwhelmed by tenderness when he realised how small and fragile they felt in his. Everything he had done had been for one reason: to protect her.

His voice was rough when he continued but it was impossible to pretend that he didn't feel anything when he felt so much. 'If I'd had any idea that you were pregnant then I would never have left. I'd have stayed and looked after you, you and our baby.'

'Out of duty,' she repeated brokenly, her eyes welling with tears.

'No. Not out of duty. Because I wanted to.' He drew her into his arms because he simply couldn't see her suffering like this and not do anything about it. Her body felt stiff at first, resisting his attempts to comfort her, and he smiled sadly. Beth could be stubborn at times but there again so could he. Maybe that was why they had been such a perfect match.

The thought seemed to unlock the final barrier as memories of their past life together came flooding back. Although he had been out with a lot of women over the years, he had never felt for them what he had felt for Beth. Marriage had never been high on his agenda but when he'd met her, he had realised that it was what he wanted more than anything. Knowing that Beth was his and that he was hers had felt like a dream come true.

For the first time in his life, he had felt that he had belonged. And then Beth had told him that what she wanted more than anything was for them to have a child and everything had changed.

Sadness welled up inside him as he recalled her heartache when she had failed to conceive and he drew her closer, wanting in some way to make up for what she had suffered. Her body felt so tense as it rested against his, every muscle taut, and his heart ached all the more.

Beth didn't deserve this! She didn't deserve to suffer any more after what she had been through. He ran his hand down her back in an attempt to comfort her, following the rigid line of her spine. When he felt a tremor pass through her, he froze, expecting at any moment that she would push him away. He wasn't prepared when all of a sudden she relaxed against him.

Callum's breath caught when he felt her breasts brushing enticingly against his chest. His hand was shaking as it moved on, feeling the tension seep out of her with each gentle stroke of his fingers. When he reached her waist and paused, she looked up, her eyes holding his in a look that shocked him to the core. Far from wanting him to stop, he could tell she wanted him to continue!

Callum could feel the blood pounding through his veins as his hand slid over the rounded curve of her bottom. Beth didn't say a word but he could feel her nestling against him and the thought that she welcomed his touch was just too much. Bending, he took her mouth in a searing kiss. Her lips felt cool at first but he could feel the heat building beneath the chill, and groaned.

The rational part of his mind knew that he should stop what was happening. Beth was upset and she wasn't thinking clearly, but how could he stop when it was what he wanted so desperately? His tongue traced the outline of her lips and he shuddered when he felt them part for him. He hadn't kissed another woman since they had met and now he understood why. He only wanted Beth: no other woman would do.

The thought filled his head as his tongue mated with hers. When he drew her down onto the rug, she didn't protest. Callum ran his hands down her body, relearning its shape and feel. She was thinner than she had been, although her breasts were fuller, filling his palms when he cupped them in his hands. Undoubtedly, it was the result of giving birth to their daughter and he loved the thought that such a momentous event had caused these changes.

Bending, he drew her nipple into his mouth, lavishing it with love through her cotton blouse, wishing with all his heart that he had been here to watch her nurse their daughter. He had missed so much that was precious, missed making so many wonderful memories. Now all he could do was pray that he wouldn't miss any more.

A chill ran through him at the thought that nothing was guaranteed but even that couldn't dampen his ardour. His body was throbbing for release, but he didn't intend to rush things. He ran his hands down her body again, caressing the sweet, lush curves, before turning his attention to the buttons down the front of her blouse. Surprisingly he managed to undo them without any difficulty and he raised surprised eyes to hers.

'I must be getting better at this,' he said, ruefully, parting the blouse so he could drop a kiss on the warm curve of her breast. 'Buttons were never my forte.'

'It must be all the practice you've had,' she said flatly, and he frowned because that wasn't what he had meant to imply.

'Nope. I can honestly say that I haven't had any practice at all.' He waggled his fingers, opting to make a joke out of it as it made him feel incredibly vulnerable to admit that he hadn't slept with anyone else since they had parted. 'I must have discovered a natural talent somehow or other.'

'Oh.'

An expression of relief crossed her face before she reached up and drew his head down, but Callum had seen it and his heart swelled with joy. Beth was pleased that he hadn't slept with anyone else and it could only mean that she still cared about him. The thought filled his head as he stripped off her blouse and tossed it aside. The plain white bra she was wearing underneath was soon dispensed with as well, along with the rest of her clothes. Callum could feel his heart racing as he stared down at her naked body.

'You're so beautiful,' he whispered, hoarsely. 'So very, very beautiful.'

Beth didn't say a word as she waited for him to remove his clothes but her eyes never left him. Callum could feel her watching him as he dragged his sweater over his head, and shuddered. It was incredibly erotic to know that she enjoyed looking at him, that she wanted him.

He was trembling when he lay down beside her and drew her into his arms, letting her feel just how much he wanted her too. When he ran his hand down her body, seeking out the source of her heat, she shuddered, her breathing turning rapid and shallow as he caressed her. Callum continued to stroke her, his own passion rising until he couldn't hold back any longer. He slid into her with one smooth powerful thrust, felt her tighten around him, and gasped. All of a sudden nothing mattered but this—he and Beth, and the magic they were creating together.

CHAPTER TEN

IT WAS ALMOST midnight when Beth awoke. At some point they had moved upstairs to the bedroom and moonlight was streaming in through the open window. She lay quite still for a moment, savouring the unfamiliar feeling of peace that filled her. What had changed? Was she now willing to believe Callum? To trust him? To accept him as part of her and Beatrix's lives?

'Penny for them. Or are they worth a lot more than that?'

Beth felt her breath catch when Callum spoke. Rolling onto her side, she let her eyes drink in the familiar planes of his face. He had changed very little in the past year, she realised. Oh, there were a few more lines around his eyes, even a touch of silver at his temples, but he was still the most handsome man she had ever seen. Although she'd had a couple of relationships before they had met, she had never felt such desire for anyone else.

Was that why she had made love with him tonight, because she'd needed the fulfilment that only Callum could give her? All of a sudden the doubts came flooding back. Was she in danger of allowing desire to cloud her judgement?

'Beth? What is it? Tell me.'

Reaching out he touched her cheek, and she flinched. The thought that she had made a mistake made her feel sick. Maybe their lovemaking had been wonderful but it hadn't changed anything—not really. Callum was still the same person he had always been, the man who had run out on her. Maybe he had claimed that he had left to protect her, left because he had cared so much about her, but did she believe him? Could she be sure that he wouldn't do the same thing again?

'Nothing.' Beth tossed back the quilt and stood

up. Picking up her dressing gown, she dragged it on, uncomfortable now with her nakedness when it just seemed to prove what a fool she had been.

'So that's it, is it?' He laughed shortly as he stood up. 'It's a bit late for second thoughts. You and I made love and there's no way that you can pretend it wasn't what you wanted, either.'

'I wasn't going to!' she retorted, hating to hear the mockery in his voice, especially when she knew that she deserved it. Callum would have stopped any time she had asked him to, but she hadn't wanted him to stop, had she? Colour flooded her face at the thought, but she refused to justify herself by lying. 'I'm as much to blame for what happened tonight as you are, Callum, but we both know it was a mistake. You and I are history and there's no way that we're going to get back together.'

'So tonight was what exactly? Some kind of nod to the past?'

'I doubt it. Let's face it, there's not a lot about

the past that either of us would want to remember.' She shrugged, aiming for a nonchalance she wished she felt. 'No, it was nothing more than a combination of circumstances. I was upset, you tried to comfort me, and one thing led to another. We're both adults, Callum. We both know that these things happen. It's nothing to get worked up about.'

'I'm glad you can be so reasonable about it,' he said flatly, pulling his sweater over his head. 'Just so long as it doesn't have a knock-on effect.'

'What do you mean by that?' Beth asked, frowning.

'That you don't use what happened tonight to stop me seeing Beatrix.' He looked her straight in the eyes. 'As you just pointed out, we're both adults and this shouldn't have any bearing on my being allowed to see her.'

'I...um...no, of course not,' Beth murmured, her heart sinking at the thought of being put on the spot this way. If she refused him access then he would think that it was because of what had happened tonight, and she didn't want that hanging over her. She wanted to forget what they had done and not be constantly reminded about it. 'You can see Beatrix whenever you want, although I don't think you need to stay here any longer now that my ankle is so much better.'

'Of course not.' Callum slipped on his shoes, his expression impossible to read in the moonlight. 'In that case, I'll sleep at the flat tonight, if that's all right with you. I'm sure we could both do with a bit of breathing space.'

'It's fine,' Beth assured him, although the thought of him moving out of the cottage was upsetting for some reason. She forced herself to focus on practicalities as it seemed safer than looking for explanations. After all, Callum had never planned to stay here on a permanent basis and she wouldn't have wanted him to, either. 'What about your clothes and everything?'

'I'll collect them tomorrow. It's a bit late to start packing at this time of the night.'

'Of course.' Beth followed him out to the landing, knowing that she should say something. 'I appreciate everything you've done for us recently. Thank you.'

He gave a little shrug. 'I was happy to help, Beth. After all, Beatrix is my daughter too.'

He didn't say anything else as he ran down the stairs and a moment later Beth heard the front door open and close again. She bit her lip as she went back into the bedroom and stared at the rumpled sheets. She could think of a dozen different reasons why she had made love with Callum tonight but in her heart she knew that only one of them was true: she had wanted him. Tears filled her eyes because now she would have to get used to being without him all over again.

Callum did his best but it was impossible to blot out the memory of that night. What made it worse was that Beth had now returned to work. With Sandra back as well, it meant that Beth was working at The Larches and it was pure torture to have to see her each day. If she had left him with even the tiniest shred of hope that their lovemaking had meant anything to her then it might have made it easier, but he didn't even have that consolation. Beth had made it perfectly clear how she felt about what had happened.

He threw himself into his work in the hope that it would help if he kept busy. The outbreak of chickenpox had spread throughout the area and the surgery was busier than ever. It was the start of the new school year and almost half the pupils were absent as so many had gone down with the virus. They were inundated with phone calls from anxious parents and, in the end, he put together an information file, explaining the symptoms and how best to treat them, and posted it on the surgery's website. It helped a bit but there were still far more people than usual requesting home visits.

They took it in turns to go out on calls and he had to admit that he welcomed the opportunity to escape from the surgery. Although Beth was unfailingly polite whenever they needed to speak, there was a definite atmosphere when they were together. Callum knew that the others had noticed it too, but, mercifully, nobody asked him what was going on. Quite frankly, he would have been hard-pressed to come up with an explanation that he wanted to share.

He was on his way to a couple of calls when Marie popped her head round his door. 'There's someone on the phone who wants to speak to you urgently,' she explained. 'I didn't catch his name because the line's terrible—that's why I didn't want to risk transferring the call to you. He did say that he was from the agency, though, if that's any help.'

'Really?' Callum exclaimed, following her back to the reception desk. He picked up the phone, wincing when he was greeted by an ear-splitting series of crackles. 'I see what you mean,' he began then stopped when someone spoke at the other end. It was a colleague from Worlds Together, the aid agency he had worked for, and his heart sank when he discovered what the other man wanted. Apparently, one of their key workers had been taken ill and they desperately needed someone experienced to take charge of their next mission: would Callum do it?

Callum hung up a few minutes later in a real quandary. Heaven only knew what Beth would say if he went flying out to Africa, even if it was only for a couple of weeks. However, if he refused to go then the trip would have to be called off and that would cause a major disruption, not to mention the loss of a great deal of money. He groaned. Talk about being stuck between a rock and a hard place!

'So how are you, Diane? Although I don't think I really need to ask you that. You're positively blooming.'

Beth drummed up a laugh as Diane Apple-thwaite sat down in front of her desk. It was the monthly antenatal clinic and Diane was her last patient that afternoon. Normally, Beth enjoyed seeing the new mums but she was finding it hard to concentrate that day and it was all down to Callum. She had bumped into him as he was on his way out to do some home visits and he had asked her if he could have a word with her when he got back. She had no idea what it was about, but, knowing what had happened the last time they had had a serious conversation, it was little wonder that her internal alarm bells were ringing like mad.

'I feel marvellous, but then I always do when I'm pregnant,' Diane assured her. 'That's prob-ably why Phil and I had so many children, al-though this little one has come as a complete surprise.'

'So how did your husband take the news?' Beth asked, trying not to think about that night. So she and Callum had made love—so what?

As she had told him at the time, they were both adults and it was nothing to get worked up about. She sighed as she unravelled the sphygmomanometer cuff so she could check Diane's blood pressure, wishing that she actually believed that. 'Was he pleased?'

'Once he got over the shock, he was.' Diane laughed. 'I don't expect Phil thought we'd have another one at our age but, as I pointed out to him, we didn't do anything to stop it.'

Beth managed to smile but there was a sinking feeling in the pit of her stomach all of a sudden. She and Callum hadn't taken precautions the other night either, so was it possible that she might be pregnant? It was hard to hide her dismay as she finished the examination and saw Diane out. Polly had been talking to one of her new mums, working out a birthing plan with her, and she looked up when she saw Diane leaving.

'Is that it then? I think Diane was our last patient.'

'I…er…yes, she was.' Beth went back into her room and sank down on the chair, afraid that her legs were about to give way. Although she had always wanted more than one child, how did she feel about having another baby in these circumstances? More importantly, how would Callum feel about it?

'Are you all right? You look awfully pale, Beth. Shall I fetch you a drink of water?' Polly offered in concern as she followed her into the room.

'I don't think water's going to help,' Beth muttered, closing her eyes in despair. How could she have been so stupid not to have thought about the risk before now? She could have done something about it if she had, taken the morning-after pill and made sure that she wouldn't get pregnant again by accident as she had done with Beatrix. Now it was far too late for that.

'Is it Callum?' Polly asked quietly. She sighed when Beth nodded. 'I thought you two were getting along all right these days, so what's he done now?'

'It's not what he's done—it's what we've both done.' Beth shook her head. 'I can't believe we were so stupid!'

'Tell me to mind my own business if you want, Beth, but if there's anything I can do to help then just say so.'

'There's nothing anyone can do,' Beth replied brokenly. She bit her lip but the need to tell someone was too strong to resist. 'Callum and I…well, we slept together a few weeks ago.'

'You did? But that's good, surely? Especially if it means you're thinking about getting back together,' Polly declared.

'We're not. It was a mistake and it should never have happened.' Beth put her head in her hands and groaned. 'The thing is that we didn't take any precautions and now I don't know if I might be pregnant.'

'Oh. I can see how awkward that would be,' Polly said, sitting down. 'Have you done a test yet?'

'No. I've only just thought about it,' Beth admitted. 'I can't believe I was so *stupid*!'

'There's no point beating yourself up,' Polly said firmly. 'You need to find out if you're pregnant first and then decide what you're going to do about it.'

'I don't think I could go through with a termination.' Beth felt tears well to her eyes. 'After everything we went through to have a child, I really couldn't do that.'

'That's something only you can decide, Beth.' Polly stood up. 'I'll go and get a pregnancy testing kit from the pharmacy.' She shook her head when Beth went to speak. 'Don't worry— I'll tell them it's for one of my mums. Nobody needs to know anything until you're sure what's happening.'

Polly hurried from the room, leaving Beth in the throes of despair. The thought that even now there might be a new life growing inside her should have filled her with joy but all she could think about was how Callum would react. While there was no doubt that he loved Beatrix, it that didn't mean he would welcome another child into his life, especially when there was no chance of them getting back together.

'Beth? Am I disturbing you? Only I need to have a word with you.'

Beth's head shot up in panic when she heard Callum's voice. 'I'm just waiting for Polly,' she said quickly, using the first excuse that sprang to mind. The last thing she needed at this moment was to have to talk to him.

'That's all right. It won't take long.' He came into the room and she felt her nerves tighten even more when she saw how serious he looked. She had a feeling that she wasn't going to like what he had to say, but before she could attempt to prepare herself, he carried on.

'There's no point me beating about the bush. The agency phoned today. They're sending a team out to Africa tomorrow but the team leader has been taken ill and is unable to go. It will cause chaos if they have to call it off at this late stage, not to mention the fact that a great deal of money will be lost if they have to re-book the flights.' He shrugged. 'Basically, I've agreed to go along.'

Callum could tell that the news hadn't gone down well but it was no more than he had expected. Beth had made no bones about her doubts as to his commitment to Beatrix and to his new life here, and this must confirm all her fears. He opened his mouth to explain that he would only be away for a couple of weeks but just as that moment Polly appeared.

'Oh, sorry! I didn't know you were here, Callum.'

She started to back out of the room but Callum beckoned her to come in. Quite frankly, he was sick and tired of being seen as the bad guy all the time: Mr Unreliable. If Beth wasn't convinced by now that he was serious about sticking around then she never would be.

'Don't leave on my account,' he said flatly, avoiding Beth's eyes. He didn't need to see the contempt they held to know it was there and the thought was so bitter that he had to wait a beat before he could continue. 'I've said what I came to say and that's it. I'll see you when I get back, Beth.'

He swung round, holding himself rigid as he made his way to his room. The urge to go back and beg her to understand that he'd had no choice in the matter was overwhelming, but he mustn't do it. Beth had to trust him. She had to know in her own heart that he would never let Beatrix down. He couldn't force her to feel that way: it had to come from inside her. And if it never happened then there was nothing he could do about it.

The thought that she might always doubt him hurt like hell but he knew that he had to accept it, somehow. He had already spoken to Daniel and received his blessing, so once he had handed Marie his notes, he left the surgery and went up to the flat. It didn't take him long to pack. He'd done it so many times before that he knew exactly what to take. Anyway, it wasn't what he was taking with him that mattered this time, but what he was leaving behind.

Callum took a deep breath, struggling to control the agony he felt. He was going to miss Beatrix so much while he was away and he was going to miss Beth too. Even if she didn't believe in him, she was the woman he loved with all his heart and it was going to be pure torture to be without her.

The test proved negative. Beth was overwhelmed with relief when she realised that she wasn't pregnant after all. After Callum's announcement, having another baby would have been a complete disaster. She told Polly the good news, cutting short her friend's attempts to talk about Callum's forthcoming absence. As far as she was concerned, there was nothing to talk about. Callum was simply behaving true to form.

The thought weighed heavily on her as she cleared up. It was her early finish so once she had collected Beatrix, she went straight home and set about the nightly routine. It was after seven before she allowed herself to think about what Callum had told her and her heart started to ache with a mixture of pain and disappointment. Even though she'd had her doubts all along about his commitment, it was still hard to face up to the fact that he had chosen his old life over their daughter.

It made her see that it would be a huge mistake to continue allowing him to have access to Beatrix. It was bad enough that he was leaving her now, but how much worse would it be the next time, when Beatrix was older and more aware of what was happening?

The thought of her daughter's confusion was more than Beth could bear. She knew only too well how it felt to be abandoned by the person you loved and she refused to let her daughter go through that kind of heartache. Once Callum came back then she would make it clear that he wasn't welcome any longer. Hopefully, he would have the sense to leave Beesdale for good then, and not put them through any more stress. Pain shot through her at the thought of never seeing him again, but she knew it was what she needed to do. It was better to put an end to it now than run the risk of Beatrix getting hurt even more in the future.

Callum couldn't sleep. He kept going over what he had said to Beth or, rather, what he hadn't said. Why in heaven's name hadn't he explained that he would only be away for a couple of weeks and that once the agency found someone else to take over, he would return to England? Why hadn't he reassured her that once he came back, he wouldn't go away again? He had already made it clear to the agency that this would be his last assignment but he had been too damned stubborn to explain all that to Beth. Too stubborn or just too proud!

He got up, pacing the floor as he tried to decide what to do. Should he go to see her and explain it all to her now? But would she listen to him? That was the question? He sighed wearily because he doubted it. Beth had made up her mind about him from the moment he had come back to Beesdale and he would be a fool to imagine that she was willing to give him the benefit of the doubt. He had left her: ergo he would leave their daughter too.

It was painful to have to face it, but what was even more upsetting was the fact that he had thought he was making some progress. Even after they had made love that night, she had allowed him to carry on seeing Beatrix, but would she let him see their daughter when he got back from this trip? He didn't think so! He would be right back to square one, and this time it would be even harder to convince her to trust him. The thought made up his mind. He had to make Beth understand why he had agreed to go.

Callum dragged on his clothes and left the flat. It was after midnight and there was no traffic about as he drove to the cottage. He drew up outside, feeling his nerves jangling when he saw that the sitting room light was on. Was Beth still up, thinking about what had happened, about the way he had seemingly confirmed all her worst fears? He knew it was true and the thought of how difficult it was going to be to make her understand why he was doing this made him feel sick. He got out of the car and knocked on the door, feeling his heart start to race when she opened it.

'I wanted to explain,' he said softly, wishing she would say something rather than stand there, staring at him.

'What is there to explain?' She smiled thinly and he winced when he saw the contempt in her eyes. 'The lure of the job proved too much to resist. It must be far more exciting working overseas than working here.'

'You're completely wrong.' Callum took a deep breath to damp down the anger that shot through him at the knowledge that she thought he was so fickle. 'I only agreed to go because they were desperate for someone to take charge. I told you, if I don't go then the trip will have to be called off and that will cost the agency a great deal of money they can't afford to lose. It's only for two weeks and then I'll be back.'

'So it's Dr O'Neill to the rescue?' Her laughter echoed with scorn. 'How wonderful it must be to know that you're such a hero.'

'I'm not a hero,' he said through gritted teeth. 'I am merely doing what I think is right.'

'And you're very good at that, aren't you, Callum?'

'Meaning?'

'Meaning that you're very good at doing what's right.' She shrugged when he didn't reply. 'You left me because you thought it was the right thing to do, and now you're going on this assignment.' She gave a harsh little laugh. 'Not many people are as sure as you that they're doing the right thing. I know I'm not.'

'I can't believe that.' It was his turn to laugh now, although there was a hollow feeling in his stomach. Nothing he said was going to persuade her to trust him. 'You seem pretty sure about me, Beth. In fact, you don't appear to have any doubts at all that you might be wrong about me.'

'You haven't given me any reason to,' she shot back.

'No? So you don't believe that I love Beatrix and want only what's best for her?' He carried on when she didn't answer. 'Don't let your feelings about what happened between us blind you to the truth. I love our daughter and I would never hurt her. I think you know that, only you're too afraid to admit it.'

There was nothing else he could think of to say. Callum drove back to the flat and fetched his bag then went out to the car. It was far too early to catch his train so he would drive down to London instead. It would be better than lying in bed, thinking about Beth and what else he should and shouldn't have said. It was down to her now, although if she thought she could use this trip to cut him out of Beatrix's life then she was mistaken.

His mouth thinned. He was going to be a proper father to his daughter—with or without Beth's blessing!

CHAPTER ELEVEN

'I THINK IT may have been a TIA,' Beth said gently, looking at the middle-aged couple sitting in front of her desk. Penny and Michael Halthorpe had been rushed into the surgery by their son. They had been at a family gathering, celebrating their twenty-fifth wedding anniversary, when Michael had been taken ill, so she could appreciate what a shock this must be for them. 'A transient ischaemic attack—a kind of mini-stroke, in other words.'

'A stroke,' Penny echoed. 'My dad had a stroke and he was never the same…' She tailed off, too upset to continue.

Beth sighed softly. Michael Halthorpe ran the local building firm and he was well known in the town. It was a family concern and his son,

Alistair, worked with him while Penny dealt with the paperwork. They were currently working on an extension to the junior school, adding an extra classroom as well as a new gymnasium.

This was going to be a blow for them on many levels and she chose her words with care. 'You said that you realised something was wrong when Michael spilled your drink—is that right, Penny?'

'Yes. We'd gone to The Fleece for lunch, you see. Everyone was there—our son, Alistair, and Cathy, our daughter-in-law, the grandchildren, Michael's parents. There was wine on the table but I wanted a soft drink so Michael went to the bar. It was as he was on his way back that I noticed he was holding the glass so that the tonic water was spilling out. Someone made a remark about him being one over the eight but I knew it wasn't that. Then when he sat down, he couldn't lift his hand up onto the table. That's when Alistair said that he'd drive us here to the surgery.'

'Which was exactly the right thing to do,' Beth assured her. She turned and smiled at Michael. 'So how do you feel now? Can you raise your arm?'

He shook his head. 'No. I keep trying but it still won't work properly.'

'Don't worry about it.' She could tell that his speech was a little bit slurred as well but, apart from that, he appeared relatively well. 'I've given you the recommended amount of high-dose aspirin and now it's simply a case of waiting for the ambulance to get here. They'll run a series of tests at the hospital to check if it was a TIA and then they'll put you on medication to prevent it happening again.'

'They can do that?' Penny exclaimed.

'They can indeed. It's very different these days from when your father had his stroke,' Beth explained. 'There's a range of medication that can and does work wonders.'

'Thank heavens.' Penny closed her eyes in sheer relief at hearing that. Michael used his good hand to reach for hers.

'You're not getting rid of me that easily,' he declared, smiling at his wife with such love in his eyes that Beth felt a lump come to her throat. Once upon a time she had thought that she and Callum had the kind of relationship that would last a lifetime but she'd been wrong. He'd got bored after only a few years of being married to her.

It was a painful thought so it was a relief when Marie knocked on the door and ushered in the paramedics. Michael and Penny went in the ambulance, with their son following on in his car. The emergency had set her back so it was way past the time she should have finished before Beth had seen everyone.

She hurried out to her car, not wanting to be late collecting Beatrix. The little girl had been very unsettled recently, crying when Beth left her each morning. Although she knew that a lot of children went through a clingy stage, Beatrix seemed very unsettled at home too and she could only put it down to one thing: her baby was missing Callum.

Beth's mouth compressed as she drove out of the surgery. Callum had been gone for three weeks now and she'd had no contact with him since he had left. It shouldn't have come as a surprise. After all, he was doing what he loved best and he didn't have time to worry about his daughter or anyone else. However, if he thought he could get away with such behaviour, he was mistaken. When he came back then she intended to make it clear that there was no place for him in Beatrix's life.

Callum had never felt so frustrated in his life. So far the agency had failed to find a replacement for him so he'd been forced to stay on far longer than he had expected. Add to that the fact that they were working in one of the remotest areas of the planet, which made communications virtually impossible, and he was consumed with impatience.

He could just imagine what Beth must be thinking. Not only had he gone haring off to the other side of the globe, but he hadn't even bothered to get in touch with her and he hadn't returned when he'd said he would. If she'd had doubts about his suitability as a parent before this, they must have multiplied a hundredfold!

When word finally came that a replacement had been found, he was overjoyed. He packed up and made the long journey back to the capital where he wasted another couple of precious days hanging around the airport after his flight was cancelled. Eventually, he was on his way and arrived back at Heathrow in the early hours of the morning. He collected his car from the car park and set off. Although it was a long drive up to Yorkshire, all he wanted was to get home.

His heart lurched as the word slid into his head. He had never really considered anywhere as home before. Being sent away to school at such a young age had made it difficult to put down roots. Even after he and Beth had married and he had moved to the Dales, he had found it hard.

However, somewhere in the past couple of months Beesdale had laid claim to him, although maybe it wasn't the town so much as the people who lived there, he realised suddenly. He had missed Beth and Beatrix so much while he had been away and he knew how empty his life would be without them. Even if Beth still had doubts about him, he had to find a way to convince her that all he wanted was to be with her and their daughter for the rest of his days.

Callum could feel his heart racing as he joined the motorway. He knew it was going to be extremely hard to make Beth trust him but he was determined to do so, determined that he would speak to her that very day. After all, she had trusted him enough to sleep with him, even though she had claimed later that it hadn't meant anything. He frowned. All of a sudden he didn't believe it. It was completely out of character for her to do such a thing. Beth would *never* have slept with him if she hadn't felt something for him!

The thought buoyed him up so that he barely noticed the miles passing. It was early morning when he reached Beesdale and there was a lot of traffic about. He slowed down as he approached the school. As well as parents dropping off their children, there was a truck delivering building materials for the new extension and he waited while it backed into the playground. Although the area around the site of the extension had been fenced off, children were entering the school through the main doors a few yards away.

Callum frowned when he saw the truck suddenly lurch backwards. To his mind, the driver was going far too fast and needed to slow down. The thought had barely crossed his mind when there was an almighty crash as the rear of the truck struck the building. Metal supports flew in all directions as they were ripped away and he gasped in horror when he saw the gable end of the old Victorian building start to give way. Huge blocks of stone began to rain down onto the playground as he leapt out of his car and ran across the road.

'Someone call the emergency services,' he shouted, running over to the truck. The cab had been partly crushed by the falling masonry and he could just make out the driver, slumped over the wheel. He climbed up to the cab and felt for the man's pulse but he couldn't find one. There was nothing he could do for him so he climbed back down and ran over to a woman who had a deep cut on her cheek. Taking a clean hand-kerchief out of his pocket, he pressed it against the cut to stem the bleeding then called over a man who was standing nearby.

'Keep putting pressure on it until the bleeding stops. It'll need stitching so make sure the para-medics see her when the ambulances get here.'

Callum moved on, checking the rest of the casualties who had been in the playground. Thankfully, nobody appeared to be badly injured, although one elderly man had a broken arm. He used a borrowed scarf to stabilise it then turned his attention to those inside the school. Some of the workmen from the site had started to clear a path to the main entrance, which had been blocked by falling stones. There was a young man directing operations and Callum hurried over to him.

'I need to get inside to see if anyone's been injured,' he explained.

'I'm not sure if that's possible,' the younger man replied. 'Some of those blocks of stone are barely holding in place and they could shift at any moment. I'm Alistair Halthorpe. It's my family's firm that is doing the building work.' He shot a worried glance at the truck. 'What about Ken, the truck driver? He and my dad have been friends for years...' He tailed off when Callum shook his head.

'Sorry. I'm afraid he didn't make it.' He waited a beat then continued, knowing that they didn't have time to grieve for the driver if they were to help the people trapped inside the building. 'Is there another way in?'

'There is, but it's in an even worse state than this.' Alistair made an obvious effort to collect himself as he led Callum around the building and pointed to what had been the back entrance. Callum's heart sank when he discovered that it had been completely blocked when part of the roof had caved in.

'There's no way you can get in that way—we won't be able to shift those beams for a start,' Alistair told him. 'We'll have to wait for the fire and rescue teams to get here. They'll have heavy lifting gear with them.'

'But how long will that take?' Callum shook his head. 'We can't afford to wait. If anyone's been seriously injured then they need help now. If we could manage to clear a passageway through the rubble then maybe I can get inside.'

They went back to the front of the building. News of what had happened had spread and there was a large crowd milling about now. More men had joined the team shifting the stones away from the entrance and Callum went to help them. It was hard going but in a fairly short time a narrow passage had been opened up. Callum ran over to his car for his bag then hurried back and knelt down. There was just enough room for him to crawl through if he was careful.

'Try not to knock against any of those stones,' Alistair instructed, handing Callum a hard hat. 'One wrong move and the whole lot could fall on top of you.'

'That's reassuring to know,' Callum replied, drolly. He eased himself forward, taking his time so that he wouldn't inadvertently set off a landslide. It was highly uncomfortable crawling over the rough surface but he kept going until he reached the end of the passageway. There was a woman there, her face grey with worry, and she helped him to his feet.

'Thank heavens!' she exclaimed. 'I didn't know how long it would be before the emergency services arrived.'

'I'm afraid they aren't here yet,' Callum told her. 'It's just me for now. I'm Dr O'Neill from the surgery. Is anyone badly injured?'

'I'm Mrs Goulding, the head teacher,' the woman informed him, leading the way along the corridor. 'A couple of the children were hit by stones but, thankfully, they're more shocked than anything else. Mr Benson is my main concern. Nick was knocked out when a lump of stone fell on him. He's regained consciousness now but he seems rather confused.'

'I'll take a look at him first,' Callum said, his heart sinking. If the man had suffered a head injury then he would need immediate treatment at the hospital.

'He's in here. I know you're not supposed to move a casualty but I was worried in case the rest of the gable end came down, so we put him in the office. One of the other teachers is with him.'

Mrs Goulding opened the door and ushered Callum inside. He went straight over to the young man propped up against the desk and knelt down. 'I'm Dr O'Neill,' he explained, opening his bag and taking out a small torch. 'Mrs Goulding tells me that you've had a bang on the head.'

'That's right.' Nick Benson winced as he touched his temple. 'Something must have hit me, although I don't really remember what happened, if I'm honest.'

Callum's heart sank that bit more when he realised how slurred the other man's speech sounded. 'How long was he unconscious?' he asked, shining the torch into Nick Benson's eyes. Although the left pupil reacted normally to the light, the right one was very sluggish, an indication that Nick had concussion.

'About five minutes, although it could have been longer,' the young woman teacher, who had been delegated to sit with him, replied shakily. 'We were more concerned about getting the children to safety, you see, so it was a while before anyone realised that Nick had been hurt.'

'I see.' Callum nodded. 'I want you to keep a close eye on him. If his condition changes in any way, i.e. he lapses into unconsciousness again or has difficulty speaking, then I want you to come and get me straight away.'

The young woman nodded, obviously appreciating the seriousness of the situation. Callum followed Mrs Goulding out of the office and along the corridor to the hall where the children were gathered. An area in the corner had been cleared and he could see half a dozen or so children sitting there, along with a couple of mothers who must have been in the school when the accident had occurred. He was surprised when he spotted Polly amongst them.

'What are you doing here?' he asked, going over to her.

'I was dropping Joseph off,' she explained,

looking equally surprised to see him. 'How about you? When did you get back?'

'First thing this morning,' Callum told her, and grimaced. 'I drove straight up here and was outside when the accident happened.'

'Does Beth know you're back?' Polly asked.

'No. I was going to surprise her, although whether it would have been a pleasant surprise is debatable,' he added wearily.

'Don't give up.' Polly smiled at him. 'No matter what Beth says, I know she cares about you, Callum. More than cares, in fact.'

Callum didn't get chance to say anything because Mrs Goulding interrupted them just then. However, as he followed the head teacher over to where a little girl was sobbing noisily, his heart was racing. Was it true? Did Beth care about him? He had no idea but he intended to find out as soon as he could.

Beth didn't hear about the accident until she went into work. Everyone was talking about it and she frowned in consternation. 'Was anyone badly injured?'

'Nobody knows yet,' Marie told her. 'Apparently, the children are still inside the school and they're having to wait for the emergency services to arrive. From what I can gather, it's too dangerous to try to get them out without the proper equipment.'

'How awful!' Beth exclaimed. 'Is there anything we can do?'

'Daniel's gone down there to find out. He said he'd phone and let us know what's happening...' Marie broke off when the telephone rang. She snatched up the receiver, listening intently to what was being said. 'That was Daniel. The fire and rescue teams have just arrived,' she explained after she'd hung up. 'They're going to shore up the building and make it safe. It appears that both entrances are blocked so they're going to get the children out through the windows.'

'Thank heavens for that.' Beth shuddered at

the thought of the children being trapped inside. 'What does Daniel want us to do? Did he say?'

'Carry on as normal. Any minor injuries can be treated here while anything more serious will need to be ferried to the hospital,' Marie told her.

'Right, that's what we'll do then.'

Beth went to her room, wondering how many people had been injured. At least the emergency services were on site now and that would help. She saw a couple of patients then attended to a little girl who had been cut on the arm when a slate had dropped off the school's roof and hit her. Thankfully, the cut wasn't deep and only required butterfly stitches to hold it together.

By midday she had seen and treated at least a dozen more minor injuries. The children and their teachers had all been safely evacuated from the building now but she decided not to go for lunch in case she was needed. She was just making herself a cup of coffee when Polly appeared.

'Have you heard about the accident?' she asked, over her shoulder.

'Yes. I was there when it happened, in fact,' Polly replied.

'Really?' Beth swung round and stared at her friend in dismay. 'Are you all right?'

'I'm fine, so's Joseph. He thought it was great fun when the fireman carried him down the ladder to get him out.'

'Where is he now?' Beth asked, frowning.

'Waiting in the car.' Polly took a deep breath then hurried on. 'I'm about to take him home but I wanted to let you know something first. Callum's still inside the school. Apparently, one of the staff has been quite badly injured and he's stayed with him.'

'Callum? But he's in Africa,' Beth protested, unable to take it in.

'He got back in the early hours of this morning and drove straight up here,' Polly explained, then shrugged. 'I got the distinct impression that he was keen to see you, Beth.'

'I doubt it,' Beth said shortly.

'Why won't you give him a chance?' Polly held up her hand when Beth opened her mouth. 'I know what you're going to say, that he let you down and you can't trust him not to do it again. But it's obvious that he cares about you otherwise he wouldn't have come haring back here as fast as he could.'

'So he cares, does he? Well, he has a funny way of showing it, that's all I can say.' Beth bit her lip when she felt tears well to her eyes. Even though she knew it was ridiculous, it had hurt to be ignored again. 'He never even bothered to contact me while he was away, not even to ask about Beatrix.'

'There could be a very good reason for that,' Polly pointed out. 'I mean, we have enough problems getting a signal at times, and we live in *Yorkshire*, not the depths of Africa!' She sighed. 'All I'm saying, Beth, is don't cut off your nose to spite your face. You'll only regret it.'

Beth picked up her mug of coffee after Polly

left and took it back to her room. Was Polly right? Should she give Callum the benefit of the doubt? She took a sip of the hot liquid, thinking back over what had happened since he had first returned to Beesdale.

He had done everything he possibly could to convince her that he was serious about wanting to be a proper father to Beatrix, hadn't he? It was obvious that he loved Beatrix and that Beatrix loved him too, so why couldn't she accept that? Why wouldn't she trust him? Because it wasn't enough to know that he loved their daughter when she wanted him to love her too? Love her as much as she loved him?

All of sudden, she could see the situation clearly. She had never stopped loving him. Even when he had told her that he'd wanted a divorce, it hadn't changed how she felt about him. Oh, she had been hurt and angry but she had still loved him. That was why she had made love with him the night Beatrix was conceived. It was also why she had made love with him a few weeks ago. She loved him with every fibre of her being and knowing how she felt terrified her.

But Callum had never set out to upset her. What he had told her was true. He had left because he had been afraid for *her*. He had only asked her for a divorce because he had honestly thought it was the best thing he could do to protect her. How blind she had been not to understand all that before!

Beth stood up, her legs shaking as she hurried from the room. She didn't bother with her car but ran out of the surgery and along the road. All she could think about was Callum trapped inside the school. From what she could gather, there was every likelihood that it would collapse, and if that happened then she might never get the chance to tell him how she felt, how much she loved him.

The thought lent wings to her feet so that it took only minutes to reach the school. Barriers had been set up to keep people away and her heart raced when she saw the grim expressions on the faces of the firemen who were attempting to stabilise the building. All of a sudden there was a warning shout and she gasped in horror when she saw the front wall of the building start to bow out. Then with a tremendous roar, it collapsed. Beth pressed her hand to her mouth. Somewhere beneath all that rubble was Callum.

CHAPTER TWELVE

CALLUM WAS CHECKING Nick Benson's vital signs when he felt the building suddenly tremble. Nick had lapsed into unconsciousness again and Callum knew how urgent it was that they get him to hospital as soon as possible. If Nick had suffered a bleed on his brain, as Callum suspected, then pressure would be building inside his skull and he would need an operation to relieve it. Although it wasn't ideal to move him in this condition, Callum knew that he had no choice. He had to find a place that would provide them with some degree of protection if the building collapsed.

Looping Nick's arm over his shoulder, he half-dragged and half-carried him out of the office. He had no idea of the layout of the school but it seemed wiser to move away from the front of the building. Nick felt like a dead weight as he hauled him along the corridor, glancing into the classrooms as he passed, but none of them were suitable. He came to the kitchen and paused. Although the worktops would afford them very little protection, there was a walk-in refrigerator that might just do the job.

Callum didn't waste any more time debating its merits. He dragged Nick across the kitchen and bundled him into the fridge, slamming the door behind them. He was only just in time too as there was a loud groaning noise followed by a mighty roar as the building collapsed. Callum could hear stone raining down all around them and flinched, expecting at any moment that they would be crushed by falling masonry.

He could scarcely believe it when the noise finally stopped and he and Nick were unharmed. Forcing open the door, he gasped when he saw the state of the kitchen. Everything had been

destroyed and it was hard to believe that the refrigerator was still intact.

Leaving Nick in the relative safety of the refrigerator, Callum squeezed out of the door. Although it would be safer to wait there until the
rescue team came to find them, he needed to
get Nick to hospital. It wasn't easy finding his
way through all the rubble and several times
he had to retrace his steps when the way ahead
was blocked, but finally he could hear voices
up ahead.

He hurried towards them, so intent on getting help for Nick that he never noticed the broken beam dangling from what remained of the
roof. He was directly underneath it when it fell,
catching him squarely across his upper back.
He slumped, face down, onto what had been the
floor, hearing the anxious voices of the rescue
team as they clustered around him.

'Nick…in the kitchen,' he managed to mur-
mur. 'In the fridge….'

Blackness suddenly rose up to claim him and

the last thing he saw before he slid into unconsciousness was Beth's face. A wave of sadness washed over him. Now he wouldn't get the chance to tell her how much he loved her.

It was the worst time of Beth's entire life. She went with Callum in the ambulance as it rushed him to hospital. Although he had regained consciousness, she wasn't able to talk to him because the paramedics were too busy checking his vital signs. All she could do was try to make sure he knew that she was there, although he was so woozy from the pain relief he'd been given that she doubted if he had registered the fact. He was taken straight to Resus and she was asked to wait outside. She paced the corridor, wondering when someone would come and tell her how he was.

It seemed like a lifetime had passed before the consultant appeared and her heart lurched when she saw how grave he looked.

'How is he?' she demanded. 'Do you know the full extent of his injuries yet?'

'No. We'll know more after he's had a scan.' The consultant led her into a side room. Beth sank down onto a chair, biting her lip as he continued. It wouldn't help if she gave in to the fear bubbling away inside her. 'As you know, the beam caught him across the upper back. There's extensive swelling in the area so it's difficult to tell how much damage has been done. I'll need to see the results of the MRI scan before I have a clearer idea.'

'So you don't know if he's suffered any spinal damage,' she said, her voice catching as she expressed her worst fear.

'No,' he replied. 'However, let's not assume the worst before we know what's going on.'

Beth stood up after he left, unable to sit there while she waited for news. Her heart caught because she couldn't bear to think that Callum might have suffered life-changing injuries. She took a deep breath, forcing down the panic.

They would cross that bridge *if* and *when* they came to it. Right now she had to stay strong for Callum's sake.

Callum tried to keep a grip on the panic that filled him as he waited for the results of the scan but it wasn't easy. The thought that he might not be able to walk again was unbearable. He tried wriggling his toes but he couldn't tell if they had actually moved or not. His body felt numb from the shoulders down, plus he was still strapped to the spinal board, which made movement virtually impossible. Footsteps approached the bed and his heart started to race as he tried to prepare himself for bad news. When a figure loomed into view, it was a moment before he realised it was Beth.

'What are you doing here?' he exclaimed.

'I came in the ambulance with you—don't you remember?' She placed her hand over his and Callum felt his heart surge with relief and a whole lot of other emotions when he felt the warmth of her fingers on his. He could feel her touching him and that had to be a good sign, surely? He was still getting to grips with that thought when she bent and kissed him on the lips then drew back.

'I love you, Callum, and no matter what happens from here on, I want to be with you.'

Callum felt a wave of despair wash over him. It was what he had longed to hear her say but the circumstances were very different now. What if she was only saying that because she felt sorry for him and thought that he was going to need looking after? The thought was more than he could bear.

'I don't need your sympathy, thank you very much,' he snapped. He could tell that she was hurt by his response but better that than her thinking that she had to sacrifice herself for his sake.

'I'm not offering you sympathy,' she said, her eyes shimmering with unshed tears. 'I'm telling you how I feel, how I've *always* felt. I love you, Callum, and that's the truth, even if you don't believe me.'

'I don't.' He smiled thinly, deliberately hardening his heart because it was what he had to do. No way would he allow her to waste her life taking care of him. 'I think you're confusing pity with love, Beth, but, no, thank you. I'm not that desperate.'

Callum felt his insides twist with pain when she turned away. He longed to call her back and apologise but how could he? If it did turn out that he wouldn't be able to walk again then there was no way on earth that he was prepared to burden her with the task of caring for him. Beth deserved better than being tied to an invalid for the rest of her days.

The thought stayed with him as he waited for the consultant to return. He tried not to dwell on it but it was impossible. So much hinged on the results of this scan. If the prognosis was poor then he would have to accept that his whole life was going to change. And if it was good news then it meant that everything he had dreamt about might come true. By the time the consultant appeared, it was little wonder that his nerves were in shreds.

'I won't waste time, Dr O'Neill,' the consultant said briskly. 'The scan has proved to be less helpful than I'd hoped. The swelling around the area has made it difficult to get a clear idea of the full extent of the injury. Whilst it doesn't appear that your spinal cord has been damaged, we will still need to be extremely careful.'

'So what happens now?' Callum asked, his heart beating up a storm at such a mixed response. While it was good news that his spinal cord hadn't been damaged, he wasn't out of the woods yet, it appeared.

'Basically, we'll treat you as though you have an unstable spinal injury,' the consultant explained. 'The last thing we want is to risk the cord being damaged so we'll keep you in until the swelling subsides. Unfortunately, it means that you'll need to remain immobile during that time, but I'm sure you understand how vital it is with an injury like this.'

Callum nodded, even though his heart had sunk at the thought of being kept in hospital. 'How long will it be before you have a better idea about what's going on?'

'As soon as the swelling goes down, we'll do a second scan. That should tell us what we're dealing with.'

It was obvious that the consultant wasn't prepared to commit himself any further than that so Callum left it there. However, he knew enough about spinal injuries to guess that any damaged vertebrae would either need to be manipulated into place or surgically repaired. It all promised to take some time and he sighed as he thought about being out of action for weeks and possibly months to come.

There was so much he wanted to do, starting with telling Beth how he felt about her, although until he was certain that he was going to make a complete recovery, he didn't intend to say anything to her. His mouth compressed. He wasn't going to blight Beth's life in any way at all.

Beth had no idea what to do. Callum had made it perfectly clear that he hadn't welcomed her declaration of love and it hurt unbearably to know how he felt. It would have been much easier to hide herself away and escape the agony of rejection, but she couldn't bring herself to do that. No matter what he'd said, Callum needed her.

In the end, she phoned the hospital and discovered that he had been moved to the high dependency unit. She spoke to the sister there but, apart from saying that Dr O'Neill was comfortable, the woman wouldn't be drawn into disclosing any further information over the phone. Beth hung up in frustration. She would have to visit Callum if she wanted to learn more, although how he would feel about seeing her was debatable. It was a distressing thought but she couldn't just abandon him. She loved him far too much to do that!

Daniel agreed immediately when Beth asked him if she could take the following afternoon off to visit Callum. Everyone had been shocked by what had happened and they were eager to help any way they could.

It was almost an hour's drive to the hospital and she grew increasingly nervous the nearer she got. What if Callum refused to see her— what should she do then? Even if he didn't want anything to do with her, *she* needed to know how he was. She made her way to HDU and was directed to a side room off the main ward.

Callum was lying flat on his back, his head and body supported by a metal frame to stop him moving. He didn't see her approaching and it was only when she stopped beside his bed that he realised she was there. Her heart leapt when she saw the light that suddenly appeared in his eyes. Was he pleased to see her, after all?

'I thought I'd come and see how you are,' she

said, quickly squashing that thought before it could run away with her.

'You shouldn't have bothered,' he said gruffly. However, the brusqueness of his tone couldn't disguise another emotion, one that made her pulse race even faster. Despite his assertions to the contrary, he *was* pleased to see her.

'It's no bother,' Beth told him quietly, drawing up a chair. She laid her hand over his, felt him flinch, and knew that it wasn't because he hated her touching him. She squeezed his fingers, feeling her spirits lift as her confidence came surging back. It appeared that she still had an effect on him, even though he was doing his best to deny it. 'I wanted to come.'

'I don't know why. I thought we'd got everything straight the other day.' The gruffness was seeping away and she smiled to herself. Callum was such a terrible liar.

'I disagree. I think there's a lot that needs sorting out, starting with what I told you.' She bent closer so she could look into his eyes, wanting there to be no mistake about what she was saying. 'I love you, Callum, and it has nothing to do with pity.'

'You're mistaken.' He closed his eyes as though he couldn't even look at her. 'Learning that I'd been injured must have come as a huge shock when you thought I was still in Africa. It's little wonder that you're confused about how you feel.'

His arrogance took her breath away. He had the nerve, the sheer *gall*, to tell her how she felt! 'I'm not confused. I know exactly how I feel, Callum, I assure you.'

'You may think you do but…'

'But nothing!' Beth felt her temper soar to dizzying heights. He was doing it again, telling her what was best for her. It was exactly the same as when he had asked her a divorce. *He* had decided that she'd needed protecting, and *he* had made the decision to end their marriage. Not once had he considered consulting her!

Bending forward, she kissed him on the lips,

a kiss that was full of everything she was feeling, from anger to desire. His face was white with shock when she drew back but she didn't intend to apologise for that. 'Does that feel as though I'm confused?'

'Beth,' he began, but she didn't let him finish as she kissed him again.

There was a moment when he went rigidly still, a moment when she held her breath, wondering if she had made a huge mistake, and then all of a sudden he was kissing her back. Beth felt a wave of relief wash over her as his mouth claimed hers. Callum couldn't pretend any longer. He couldn't pretend that he didn't want her when she could *feel* and *taste* his desire.

They were both breathless when they drew apart, both aware that the truth couldn't be denied any longer. Beth could hear her voice trembling as she repeated what she had told him but this was an earth-shattering moment for both of them.

'I love you, Callum. I've always loved you and that's the truth.'

'I love you too, so much.' He broke off, overcome by what was happening. His voice was husky when he continued, filled with all the love he had tried so hard to deny. 'I never stopped loving you, either, Beth. Asking you for a divorce was the hardest thing I've ever had to do, but I was so sure that it was the only way to protect you.'

'I know.' Tears filled her eyes but they were tears of joy rather than sadness. 'I understand why you did it now, although at the time...' She broke off, not wanting to spoil everything by admitting how devastated she had been.

Callum obviously knew what she was thinking because he sighed heavily. 'I'll always blame myself for not finding a better way to convince you that we had to stop trying for a baby.'

'I doubt if there was any other way,' she admitted, sadly. 'Like you said, I was obsessed by the idea of us having a child and I couldn't think about anything else.'

'It was your dream, Beth, so don't blame yourself. Being a mother was what you wanted more than anything and I understood that.'

'It wasn't just becoming a mother that I wanted so desperately,' she said simply. 'It was having *our* baby, Callum, living proof of how much we loved each other.'

'Oh, sweetheart. That's why Beatrix means so much to me too. She's the embodiment of our love for one another.'

There were tears in his eyes now. Beth wiped them away then pressed a gentle kiss to his eyelids. That Callum had lowered his guard to this extent was incredibly moving. He had always seemed so in control of his emotions before and it was a revelation to know that he felt so deeply about her and their precious daughter.

'She's our own little miracle,' Beth said softly.

'She is.' He smiled up at her, all the love he

felt shining in his eyes. 'I love her so much, Beth, just as I love you.'

'And we love you too. That's why I'm here. I want you to know that no matter what happens, we'll always love you.'

He closed his eyes. 'I'd made up my mind that I wouldn't ruin your life if it turned out that I couldn't walk again. That's why I said what I did.'

'The only way you'll ruin my life is by shutting me out,' she said firmly. 'I want to be with you, Callum, through the good times and the bad.'

'Thank you, although maybe there aren't going to be bad times as I feared.' He quickly explained what the consultant had told him and she gasped.

'But that's wonderful! Once the damage to your spine has been repaired then you should be fine.'

'It could take some time,' he warned her. 'And I could still have limited mobility at first...'

'It doesn't matter how long it takes. You're going to get better and that's the most important thing,' she insisted.

Callum laughed. All of a sudden the future that had seemed so bleak a short time before was filled with hope. 'You're right. I will get better because I have the best incentive in the world.'

'Do you indeed?' she said, teasingly.

'I do. ' He smiled up at her, wishing with all his heart that he could sweep her into his arms but that would have to wait. For now. 'I have you and Beatrix in my life. And there can't be a better incentive than that.'

One year later...

It was like a case of déjà vu, Callum thought as he followed Daniel into the church. When he had first returned to Beesdale, he had come to the church and he could still remember the panic he had felt at the time. But today it was very different. Today there was no panic, just a deep sense of joy.

Callum took his place in the pew, thinking about what had happened in the past year. Finding out that he had a daughter had been a major event; it had changed his life for ever. He adored Beatrix and knew that she had accepted him as part of her life. One of his proudest moments had been when she had called him Dada for the first time. Although his contract as a locum had ended, Daniel had offered him a partnership when he had returned to work and Callum had eagerly accepted. He loved working in Beesdale and didn't want to work anywhere else.

The organist suddenly struck up the 'Wedding March' and the congregation rose to its feet. Callum rose as well and turned to watch Beth walking down the aisle towards him. She was holding Beatrix's hand and his heart overflowed with love when he saw them.

Although his recovery from his injuries had been frustratingly slow, Beth had been at his side every step of the way. Callum knew that he wouldn't have coped nearly as well if she hadn't been there to love and encourage him. Now he was ready to live his life to the full, a life that he would share with Beth and their daughter. They were the two people he loved most in the entire world and he couldn't believe how lucky he was to have them.

Beatrix suddenly spotted him, her face breaking into a huge smile as she pulled free and ran to him. Callum swung her up into his arms and kissed her then turned to smile at Beth. 'So you didn't change your mind,' he said softly, loving her with his eyes as he would love her with his body later.

'No. I won't ever change my mind, Callum. You're stuck with me for ever.'

'Good.' He dropped a kiss on her mouth, uncaring that everyone was watching them. They had come so close to losing one another and the thought was unbearable. They belonged together—him, Beth and their precious daughter.

Turning, he looked at the people who had come to help them celebrate this special day. They had welcomed him into their lives, made him feel part of their community, and he would always be grateful to them because it was the most wonderful feeling to know that he had found his rightful place in the world at last.

Polly was there, cradling little Angelica, with Elliot and Joseph sitting either side of her. Eleanor was keeping tight hold of Mia to stop her running to Daniel, who was Callum's best man. Diane and Phil Applethwaite had brought baby William to the church and were sitting next to old Arnold Brimsdale and his wife.

Nick Benson, now fully recovered from his injuries and back teaching, was in the next pew, along with Michael and Penny Halthorpe. Michael had handed over the family's building firm to his son and retired. Callum guessed that Michael's recent health scare allied to the death of his old friend, Ken, had made him reassess his priorities, especially when the postmortem had shown that Ken had suffered a massive heart attack while he was driving the truck that day.

Owen Walsh was there as well, sitting next to his wife, Abby. Callum had no idea if Owen had ever asked Beth out on that date because it no longer mattered. However, he was pleased that Owen and Abby were trying to make their marriage work. Having just gone through the process himself, he only hoped they would achieve the same result.

He smiled as he turned back to Beth, took hold of her hand and lifted it to his lips.

'What are we waiting for? Let's do this!'

* * * * *

LET'S TALK
Romance

For exclusive extracts, competitions and special offers, find us online:

f facebook.com/millsandboon

⌾ @millsandboonuk

🐦 @millsandboon

Or get in touch on 0844 844 1351*

For all the latest titles coming soon, visit millsandboon.co.uk/nextmonth

*Calls cost 7p per minute plus your phone company's price per minute access charge